As the closing credits rolled across on the screen, Cal leaned closer to Sue. "Funny how things worked out, huh?"

"It's hard to believe, that's what it is." When Cal had called her on Friday night, he'd suggested a trip to the drive-in. It seemed innocent enough. But now here they were. Alone in the dark. She didn't expect the effect it would have on her pulse.

"I've been thinking about this date all day," Cal whispered, just inches from her lips. "Is this what you had in mind when you agreed to go to the drive-in?"

"Actually, no..." Sue smiled.

"No?" he drawled. His lips brushed her jaw, his tongue flicked at a spot under her ear. "Then what were you thinking about?"

Susan could only sigh for an answer. Cal chuckled softly.

"So what do you say, Susan? Want to go parking?"

whose grandchildren lived in Houston. She'd missed living

Dear Reader,

Is there someone in your family or circle of friends who's the go-to person? You know, the person who can be counted on to get things done? For me, it's always been my older brother Gary. In the Riddell family, it's Cal.

Cal—or Junior, as he's known by most—has never dodged a responsibility in his life. He sits at his father's bedside at the hospital. He makes sure the bills are paid, checks on his brothers and listens to people complain. In short, Junior's the type of man I've always admired. He's solid and dependable and smart. Of course, it doesn't hurt that he's six-foot-three, with black hair and gray eyes…and has that kind of slow Texas drawl that curls a girl's toes.

I knew he'd have to find a special woman, and I think Susan Young fits the bill. She's an Ohio transplant raising a son who was recently diagnosed with diabetes. She's gorgeous and smart and more than a little stressed. And just independent enough to not be in any hurry to be "managed" by Junior.

Their relationship pulled at my heart, made me smile and made me cheer a bit, too. I've always been a sucker for a happy ending. I hope you enjoy their romance, as well.

And, I hope you'll return back to the Riddell Ranch for Trent's story in *My Christmas Cowboy.* His romance takes everyone by surprise!

Happy reading!

Shelley Galloway

My True Cowboy

SHELLEY GALLOWAY

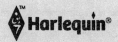

TORONTO NEW YORK LONDON
AMSTERDAM PARIS SYDNEY HAMBURG
STOCKHOLM ATHENS TOKYO MILAN MADRID
PRAGUE WARSAW BUDAPEST AUCKLAND

Recycling programs
for this product may
not exist in your area.

ISBN-13: 978-0-373-75370-3

MY TRUE COWBOY

Copyright © 2011 by Shelley Sabga

ABOUT THE AUTHOR

Shelley Galloway grew up in Houston, Texas, left for college in Colorado, then returned to Dallas for six years. After teaching lots and lots of sixth graders, she now lives with her husband, an aging beagle and barking wiener dog in southern Ohio. She writes full-time. To date, Shelley has penned more than thirty novels for various publishers, both as Shelley Galloway for the Harlequin American Romance line, and as Shelley Shepard Gray for Avon Inspire.

Her novels have appeared on bestseller lists. She won a Reviewers' Choice Award in 2006 and a Holt Medallion in 2009. Currently, she writes all day, texts her son at college too much, and tries not to think about her daughter going to college next year, too. Please visit her online at www.Harlequin.com or her website, www.shelleygalloway.com.

Books by Shelley Galloway

HARLEQUIN AMERICAN ROMANCE

Don't miss any of our special offers. Write to us at the following address for information on our newest releases.

Harlequin Reader Service
U.S.: 3010 Walden Ave., P.O. Box 1325, Buffalo, NY 14269
Canadian: P.O. Box 609, Fort Erie, Ont. L2A 5X3

To Carole, a very fine woman
who's taught me a lot.

Thank you so much for all your help!

Chapter One

Cal Riddell Jr. hated hospitals. He hated how he didn't have a single ounce of control in the way they were run. Take how Electra Community was set up, for example—the place was designed like a rat's maze. It took forever to get anywhere, and half the time he got lost.

He hated the constant noise of the building, too. Metal carts squeaked and clanked as they rolled along the sterile linoleum floors. Doctors and nurses rushing down the halls. And the persistent hum and beeping of various monitors and machines. All of it pressed on his nerves something fierce.

The smell was bad. Without a doubt, the whole place reeked like gas station bathrooms and disease, all covered up with a hefty dose of disinfectant. It was a far cry from his preferred place to work—a converted tack room in the main barn back at the Riddell Ranch.

But most of all, Cal hated that his dad was in the hospital and there wasn't one thing he could do about it.

"I'm fine, Junior," his father snapped. "Do not go get me another glass of water." With an impatient glare, he added, "I told you, I'm not thirsty. Something wrong with your hearing?"

"No, sir." Cal strived for patience, but he was losing ground, fast. From the moment Cal had arrived four hours ago, his father had been especially cranky and bullheaded. Though this behavior wasn't all that new, Cal wasn't used to being the main recipient of his father's temper. He had always prided himself on being the son who was responsible and courteous.

Until very recently, it had gotten him pretty far in life. "The nurses said you needed to drink more liquids."

"Dammit, Cal. I'm sixty-two years old, not ninety-two. If I want to sip some water, I can get it myself. Without your help. But I don't want it. So stop sticking that cup in my face."

Cal put the pitcher of water aside and wished one of his brothers would appear at the door and take his place. The old coot could get him riled up like nobody's business in two seconds flat. "Fine."

Faded blue eyes flashed. "Damn right it's fine. Now, stop fussing. You're acting like an old woman. Fact is, I don't even know why you're here. You should be back at the ranch, making sure everything's running right."

"Everything is." Cal knew for a fact it was. He'd been at his desk at four-thirty that morning, checking on the latest financial holdings and making sure nothing had blown up overnight. After that, he'd joined two of the hands in the barn and helped load up the truck with supplies to take out to the north pasture.

At the moment, his BlackBerry was in his pocket, collecting emails and voice messages. He'd check in and take care of business the second he had a spare moment. Really, nothing was going to happen that he didn't know about.

But his father was oblivious. Ever since Cal had begun to take on more and more responsibility for the ranch's vast financial holdings, the old guy had asked less and less about the usual day-to-day business. Now Calvin Sr. was more likely to be riding his horse or hanging out with one of his cohorts.

That's why, instead of looking reassured, his dad just looked skeptical. "Sure?"

"Positive." As his father shifted and studied the ceiling, Cal eyed him once again. He was looking thinner. His cheeks looked sunken in, and he was agitated, too. Cal didn't blame the guy. Sitting in bed, waiting for surgery, was a horrible way to spend a day. "Want to watch some television? Maybe there's a game on."

"Doubt it." But a flicker of interest in his eyes belied his negative words.

"Let's check, just in case." Needing something to do, Cal picked up the remote and turned the TV on. Cartoons blared back at them.

His father let loose a steady stream of profanities. "Turn that thing off and get on out of here, would you? Don't know why you're even here."

"You are having surgery tomorrow, Dad. Of course I'm going to be here."

"Jarred's not. Neither is Trent."

"Trent is on tour with the rodeo. And Jarred was here yesterday before he and Serena left for their vacation in Mexico."

When Jarred had returned home, Cal learned that their father had spewed out a steady stream of abuse to Jarred for eight hours straight. And though his older brother had acted disappointed that he hadn't been able to either change the date or get a refund for his vacation in the Mexican Riviera, Cal thought it was basically all talk. More than likely, Jarred was doing everything he could to convince Serena to take even more time off at the library just so they could stay out of sight even longer.

Cal didn't blame Jarred. Not really. Fact was, their dad was difficult. And, well, a man could only take so much.

The door opened, preventing his dad from continuing his tirade.

Thank the Lord.

In clanged one of those metal carts, with a pair of nurses in tow. "Hello, Mr. Riddell," the first nurse said, a pretty gal named Rachel. "We're here to draw some blood."

His dad crossed his arms protectively over his chest. "The hell you are. You already took blood today."

"Dad, watch your mouth."

"All I said was hell." One eye fixated on Rachel. "Are you offended?"

A shy smile lit her features. "You haven't managed to offend me yet, Mr. Riddell. Even though you sure have tried."

His dad turned to him. "See?"

But all Cal saw was that it was only a matter of time before his father alienated half the hospital staff. For some reason, he felt responsible for that.

Fact was, some days he was just really tired of being his father's keeper. "I'm real sorry, Rachel," he murmured.

"Don't worry about a thing, Junior," she said softly. "He's nothing I can't handle." Then, turning to his father, she raised her voice and held out a hand. "Mr. Riddell, I'm afraid I have my orders. We need more blood. Can you hand me your arm, please?"

To Cal's embarrassment, his father told her exactly where she could put that needle.

But instead of running away, Rachel grinned and winked. "You're not scaring me away. I'm still here, Mr. Riddell. And I'm still going to take this blood."

"My heart's about to collapse, as it is. Don't see why—"

Cal looked over at the other nurse. So far, she hadn't

said a word, just stood next to the cart as if she was afraid the thing would roll off without her.

Poor thing. "Dad, enough," he said. "These nurses need to do their jobs."

"Heck, I haven't even gotten started."

Cal was just about to find a gag for his father, when Rachel turned to him again. "It looks like we're going to be here for a little while. Why don't you go take a break."

"I can stay if you need me." The only time his father had been a good patient was when he was sedated. Cal liked Rachel, and felt too sorry for the mute one to have her put up with his dad without help.

To his surprise, Rachel's smile brightened. "Things will be better if you're gone."

"Are you sure? Because I can—"

"Cal, you heard the woman. Get out of here!"

"Fine." Cal walked out just as his father started cursing everyone in the room again. He hesitated for a moment, but continued when he heard Rachel chuckle and his dad settle down.

Obviously that nurse was right. Things were going better without him in the room…perhaps because Rachel was as aware as Cal what his dad's real problem was.

Plain and simple, his father was scared to death. His years on the rodeo circuit, followed by even more years of hard living and next to no regard for food of any nutritional value had made his arteries plug up. He was due for a bypass at 7:00 a.m. and Dr. Williams had been pretty clear that he was worried about his patient's blood pressure.

He'd also told Cal that his dad was likely going to need weeks of recuperation and therapy afterward. And a lot of help.

It was a hard pill to swallow for a man who'd lived his

life on his own terms. So, to Cal, his father's mood was understandable. But, boy, was he tough to deal with.

Aimlessly, Cal wandered down the hall and caught the elevator down to the cafeteria. Two dollars bought a cup of coffee and a stale chocolate-chip cookie.

He sat near the window and slumped. What was he going to do if his dad wasn't okay? He'd been the rock in their lives. The standard to which he and his brothers all tried to measure up. What was he going to do if the old guy didn't get better?

"Excuse me. Do you mind if we sit here with you?"

Cal looked at the redhead standing in front of him, her hands full of a tray packed with enough food to feed a small village. Next to her stood a little boy about seven. "Why?"

Without waiting any longer, she set her tray on the table. "Because we're starving and there's no room anywhere else. You don't mind, do you?" she asked, sitting right down and pulling out a chair for the boy before Cal even had a moment to answer. "I mean, you've got this whole table all to yourself."

The way she was talking, you'd think he was holding up prime retail property. But as Cal looked around, he saw that she had a point. Somehow the place had gotten packed—mostly with uniformed personnel. There wasn't a spare seat to be found.

That brought him up short. Exactly how long had he been sitting there, looking out the window?

When their eyes met again, she tilted her head to one side. "You really don't mind, do you?"

He shook his head no but couldn't help ribbing her a bit. "What would you have done if I said I did?"

"I would've moved, of course."

"Really?"

She smiled, and Cal suddenly became aware of how beautiful her mouth was. "Really. But we wouldn't have been happy about it, would we, Hank?"

Hank shook his head but didn't answer. 'Course, it would have been hard for the kid to do that because there was half a hot dog in the boy's mouth.

Cal sipped his coffee and grimaced.

"You picked a bad time to get coffee," she murmured.

"Pardon me?"

She leaned closer, bringing with her the faint scent of gardenias. "It's three o'clock. New pots are always brewed at five," she whispered as though she was divulging something top secret. "You got the old stuff."

Put that way, his drink now tasted worse than ever. "Huh."

Her pretty green eyes flashed as if he'd said something interesting. "Next time, wait two hours. It's worth it. I promise."

He hoped to God there wouldn't be a next time. "Thanks for the tip."

"Sure." She picked up her fork and dug into a plate of baked ziti. "Have you ever had this? It's great."

"No."

"You should. Lucinda—she's the head chef—she fancies herself to be Italian. She really can make great pasta."

In spite of himself, he was caught in her conversation. "Fancies herself to be? You mean she's not?"

She grinned at Hank, who grinned right back as he stuck a straw into his carton of chocolate milk. "Heck, no! She's Mexican. Grew up in Acapulco." While he processed that, she turned all dreamy-eyed. "Doesn't being from Acapulco sound exotic?"

"No."

"Why not?" Hank blurted. "Lucinda says there's cliff divers there. Have you ever dived off a cliff?"

"No."

"Well, do ya want to?"

"No."

Hank wrinkled his nose and snorted, "Mister, can't you say anything but no?"

"Can't you ever shut up?"

Hank stilled and sneaked a worried look at his mom. "Uh-oh."

She glared at Cal. "We don't say 'shut up.'"

"I do. If you don't want to hear it, don't sit with me."

Instead of being cowed, the boy grinned even wider. "You've got something on your shirt! It looks like dog poop." Then the boy hopped up and scurried over toward one of the napkin dispensers.

Stunned to silence, Cal slowly looked down at his front and spied a two-inch-long slab of goo smeared right over his heart. Hastily, he grabbed a napkin and swiped.

But all that seemed to do was set the stain in worse.

Tentatively, he examined what he'd been able to get off with the napkin. Shoot. It probably was poop—but of the horse kind. When he'd helped the hands load up boxes, one of the boxes had come from an old stall. From an old stall that hadn't been properly mucked. Great. He'd been decorated with it all day long.

But everyone else had been too well-mannered to speak of it.

"Shoot. It probably is crap." He was just about to explain the stain, when he noticed the woman was staring at him, and not a bit of her expression was pleasant. In fact, that redhead could've breathed fire, she looked so pissed off.

"You know, someone really should have washed your mouth out a time or two," she blurted.

What Red didn't know was that for pretty much the entirety of his fourth-grade year, he and a bar of Dial had been best friends. Of course, that bar of soap had been his mother's doing. Everyone knew she'd been doing the best she could with three rambunctious boys.

What was this gal's excuse for her son's mouthy ways?

"Maybe someone should have taught that boy of yours some manners."

"Someone? As in me?" Her eyes narrowed. "You have a lot of nerve."

He'd had enough. Enough of being jabbed with questions. Enough of sitting in the cafeteria stewing and worrying. "Look. Just because you came over here and sat down doesn't mean I wanted to talk to you. I didn't, you know."

She had the gall to bat her eyelashes. "And here I thought you were just shy. Don't worry, I won't bother you again."

"Good." And because she was still staring at him with those sparkling eyes—and because he even noticed them—he continued, "Just so you know, I think what you're doing is shameful."

"And what is that?"

"You're obviously trying to pick me up. In a hospital. With your son in tow."

"Is that right?"

"Hell, yes."

Actually, he hadn't really thought that…he'd just been trying to get her to leave him alone. But now that he was warming up to the idea, Cal began to think it had merit. After all, she wouldn't be the first woman to cozy up to him because he was a Riddell. Lots of women had gotten close with either him or his brothers in order to get the life they'd always dreamed of having. Even Christy, who he'd thought was different.

Red was prevented from replying because Hank returned, a hunk of napkins clutched in his hand. "Hank, sit down and eat, please," she murmured.

The boy sat. But instead of picking up the rest of that hot dog, he pushed a napkin Cal's way. "I brought you a napkin for your shirt."

"Thank you."

Green eyes the same shade as his mother's watched him swipe at his shirt again. Then he spoke. "How come you're at the hospital?"

Though he hadn't intended to say another word, he said, "My dad's fixin' to have heart surgery."

"I'm here for testing," Hank said, lifting up his left hand. Two ID bracelets were wrapped around his wrist. And two tiny bruises decorated the back of his hand. Obviously the kid had had an IV lately.

Cal was taken aback. Here he'd been so focused on his own source of pain and aggravation, he'd forgotten to look around a bit. "I'm, uh, sorry."

Completely oblivious to the tension between the two adults, the boy said, "My mom's name is Susan. Susan Young."

Cal nodded in her direction. "Pleased to meet you." Though he wasn't pleased at all. Not by a long shot.

"We just moved here from Ohio. We had to move 'cause we need more money."

Cal pocketed that little bit of information all while noticing that finally Ms. Susan Young didn't look quite so smitten with her pain-in-the-ass son. "Is that right?"

"Uh-huh," Hank muttered. "Who are you?"

"Cal Riddell. Junior."

Before he stopped himself, he held out his hand and

shook hers. Carefully, he curved his palm around hers. She had a slender hand with long fingers and long pale pink nails with little rhinestones at the tips of each.

Hank screwed up his face. "Junior's your last name?"

"No, Riddell is." He waited a moment, waited for the significance of his last name to register. But neither boy nor woman so much as blinked.

After Hank swallowed another bite, he said, "So are you Cal or Junior?"

That boy could try the patience of a saint. "Both. I'm named after my dad, so most people just call me Junior."

"I'm Henry, but everyone calls me Hank instead. I like Hank. I hate Henry. What do you like being called?"

Cal had never taken the time to analyze that. Actually, no one had ever given him a choice. "Cal."

When Hank looked to be preparing to ask another twenty questions, Susan placed a hand on her son's shoulder. "Hush, now. Mr. Riddell is leaving. He doesn't want to talk to us."

Perversely, now he wasn't in such an all-fired hurry to leave.

But it was time to go. He stood up and grabbed his mug and uneaten snack. "Goodbye."

As Hank waved a free hand, Susan replied, "Goodbye to you, too. And don't worry—I'll make sure I never make the mistake of sitting anywhere near you again."

If he was in a different situation, he might have tried to smooth things over. If he was a different man, he might have apologized for his remark about her coming on to him.

If he wasn't so worried about his father, he would have apologized for swearing in front of her, too. His mother had been a good woman, and she and that bar of Dial had taught him better than that.

But at the moment, he wasn't anything but what he was. So, with that in mind, without another word, he turned and walked away.

And hardly thought about looking back at Susan and Hank Young at all.

SUSAN WATCHED THE COWBOY walk off and wondered how it was possible for a man to look so good and be such a jerk, all at the same time.

"What that man needs is an attitude adjustment," she muttered.

Hank picked up a carrot stick and bit off the top as he swiveled around to look at the cowboy's retreating form. "He sure was grumpy."

"You're right about that. Oh, well. He's not our problem. All we can do is hope his dad feels better soon."

Something changed in her son's expression, and Susan wished she could bite her tongue. Now that her boy was seven, he'd taken to letting her know often that he wasn't real happy about his fatherless state.

Telling him that he didn't need a daddy wasn't doing much good, either.

Of course, neither would telling him the truth, that his dad was little more than a glorified sperm donor. He'd moved on to another girl before Susan had even known she was pregnant. But when she did know and told him about it, he'd simply moved farther away, most likely to another willing woman's arms.

Boy, she'd made a big mistake with him.

Clearing her throat, she tapped the container of sugar-free pudding he'd insisted on having. "Why don't you finish up so someone else can have our seats."

Obediently, the boy pulled back the foil top and licked it. "I'm not all that hungry now."

If they were home, she would have fussed. But her nerves were already frayed just by being at the hospital. And by the cantankerous conversation with Cal Riddell. "All right. So are you ready to go pick out a movie to watch this afternoon?"

Hank shrugged. "I guess. But I'm getting tired of being here. I want to go home. Remember you said you were gonna paint my new room blue?"

"I remember. I can still do it next week, you know."

"But I don't wanna wait until then."

His voice had just a touch of a whine to it. Which made her think about that cowboy's comments. And how Hank did seem to be more than a little bit mouthy. "Mind your manners, Henry."

He sighed and pushed his food around on his plate. Then he said, "I still don't want to wait so long. You promised we'd paint this week."

"I don't have time. I'm here with you and working." And that was literally all she'd been doing. Working at the Lodge, or taking care of Hank. "Sometimes we don't always get what we want, son."

He rolled his eyes as he hopped off his chair and walked to throw his napkin in the trash. "I've heard that before."

Holding his tray, Susan followed slowly behind. It was hard to see resignation fill his expression time and again, but no matter how hard she was trying, Susan knew she wasn't going to make everything with him all right.

Somehow he'd still gotten diabetes.

The adjustment to Texas still wasn't going all that well, even though she'd promised Hank that things would be better for them real soon. The hospital, while state-of-the-art, was no match to Cincinnati Children's.

And now that she'd moved so far away from her parents and brother and sister, she had no one to help her with Hank.

After tossing the last of his lunch in the trash can, she led Hank back to his room.

"I wish we weren't here, Mom," he said quietly before he walked inside.

"I know." What she didn't dare add was that a lot of times, she wished they'd never moved to Texas, too.

Chapter Two

Two days later, Susan was back at work and was dividing her time between performance evaluations, hiring teenagers to work as servers in the dining room and listening to way too many complaints about other coworkers.

Now, with just one hour left of her day, she breathed a sigh of relief. It was time to play gin rummy with Rosa Ventura. After a brief knock at her partially open door, she peeked into her room. "Want to play cards today, Mrs. Ventura?"

The older woman, confined to a wheelchair for most of the last three years, looked up from the pile of newspapers by her side. "Who's playing?"

"Just me."

She looked Susan over, the way she always did, as if trying to determine if she was a worthy opponent. "All right, I guess. Care to bet?"

"Of course." Susan shook the Mason jar of pennies she'd just fished out of her locker. "I came prepared."

"If you can get a table away from that crazy Stan and find us two cups of coffee, I'll meet you in the main room in five minutes."

"I'll do my best," she said with a smile. She didn't need to ask who Stan was. The man who'd lost a leg in World War II and his pleasant disposition around 1972 was Rosa's archenemy at the retirement home. The two disagreed on just about everything, but couldn't seem to help egging each other on.

Susan had a feeling there was more to their relationship than simple dislike. After all, never were the disagreements about anything too meaningful. Yesterday an argument had erupted about the original seven Crayola colors. Last week it was the order of the first twenty presidents of the United States. That one had gotten so noisy Susan had been called in to mediate…and then had gotten a pounding from both of them when she admitted she'd never memorized all the presidents' names.

Most staff members were afraid of both Stan and Rosa. Susan agreed each was intimidating in his or her own way. But, well, she'd been through harder things, so she took their behavior in stride.

Susan shook her head as she entered the large community room of the Electra Lodge. She really would have thought at this point in their lives the two of them would have learned that there were far more important things to worry about.

She sure did. Every fifteen minutes, she'd been checking to see if the lab at the hospital had called and left a message. The wait for Hank's latest test results seemed to be taking forever. His insulin levels were high, so she was going to need to readjust his diet and medication once again.

At home, she was trying to put a positive spin on things. However, the reality was that she was still feeling guilty for Hank even having diabetes in the first place. No matter how many doctors or nurses said it had nothing to do with his lifestyle or diet, Susan was sure her crazy work schedule and single parenting was at fault.

After claiming the back game table, Susan pulled out

the deck of cards and set her jar down. She'd just filled two coffee cups when Kay Lawson, her boss, stepped in.

"How are things going today, Susan?"

"Just fine. Mrs. Ventura and I are about to play cards."

"Uh-oh. I have a feeling you're about to get soundly beaten. Again. Didn't I see the two of you playing cards yesterday?"

"Yes. We are having ourselves a rematch."

Kay grinned as she looked at her notebook. "Already I can't imagine what we would do without you here. You've sure livened things up."

"I try." Not wanting her boss to think she hadn't been doing her real job, too, she said, "I put a report on your desk about the new hires for the dining room."

"I saw it. Thank you."

"And I think the nurses on the second floor have figured out their schedules now."

Kay patted Susan's shoulder. "I didn't stop by to check on you. Just to say hello."

Susan bit her lip. Once again, she was letting her experience with the administrator in Ohio cloud her relationship with Kay.

When her old boss had hired her, she had seemed to have no problem with Susan. However, soon afterward, Susan felt as though she'd somehow landed on the director's bad side.

She'd begun to get reprimanded for not putting in enough hours, though she already worked more than the forty hours in her contract. Then other minor offenses had been written down.

Finally, Susan had known it was time to move on. She'd been very thankful when the employment recruiter had told her about Kay Lawson and the Electra Lodge. Against her family's wishes and Hank's complaints, they'd moved away from the big city and to the small Texas town.

And she'd been right. Things here really were better, work wise. Kay was a dream to work for, polite and dedicated, and appreciative of Susan's efforts.

It was just that everything else in Electra wasn't so hot. Hank wasn't making a lot of friends at school, and was already complaining about after-school day care.

And then there was the hospital. Everything just seemed to move at a slower pace. She was constantly waiting for test results or for nurses to call her back with answers to her questions.

"Well, good luck with the game," Kay said, bringing Susan back to the present. "Who knows? Maybe someone will want to take Rosa on besides you."

"I doubt that." There wasn't a person in the home who wanted to play cutthroat gin rummy the way she and Rosa Ventura did.

Just as Kay walked away, Susan spied the topic of their conversation at the entrance to the room. "I've got us a spot over here," Susan said brightly. "Let's get started."

Rosa wheeled her way to the back table. As soon as they were in whispering distance, she murmured, "Is everything okay?"

"Oh, sure. She was just checking in."

"You looked so serious. For a moment I was worried that it was about your son."

"It really was nothing. Hank's doing okay."

Rosa rubbed her hands together. "All righty, then. Let's get started before Stan comes around."

"Yes, let's definitely do that."

As Rosa started dealing, the elderly lady looked Susan up and down. "Are you sure you're all right? Something about you looks different today."

"I'm fine." She picked up her cards. "Let's just concentrate on our hands, shall we?"

But instead of accepting Susan's efforts to move them on, the older lady grimaced. "Don't you start talking to me like I don't have a brain in my head, Susan Young."

"I wouldn't dare."

"You better not, you hear me? You're one of the few people in this place who treats me like I still have my wits about me. A couple of the nurses here talk to me like I'm in kindergarten. Yesterday, at dinner, one of them asked if I needed help cutting my chicken."

Susan hid a smile at that. She wouldn't dare ask Rosa if she needed help cutting meat. At least, she wouldn't if there was a knife nearby!

As she sat across from her at the card table, Susan fiddled with her cards. "Just so you know, I really do like playing cards with you. I don't look at it as a task. I promise I don't."

Reaching out, the elderly woman patted Susan's arm. "I know, honey. Now, let's play before I lose my eyesight."

They ended up playing four games over the next hour. Susan won a hand, Rosa won the next two, and as they played the fourth round, the tension between them intensified as their competitive spirits took control. As always, they concentrated on their latest cards as if their lives depended on it. A little crowd gathered around and cheered them on.

Susan was just about to draw another card when Rosa called out, "Gin!" and slapped her cards on the table victoriously.

Susan leaned back against her chair and sighed. "One day I'm going to beat you, fair and square."

"I won't hold my breath," Rosa retorted, but there was a

bright light in her eyes that hadn't been there when Susan arrived. "Same time tomorrow?"

"I don't know if I can. I have some work I need to do on the computer that might take a while."

"Friday?"

"I can't Friday, either. I'm, uh, taking the day off."

"Susan Young, I know it's Labor Day weekend, but are you taking vacation already? Or are you finally going to tell me what's got you so stressed and worried?"

"I'm not taking vacation...." Though she was tempted to leave it at that, the concern in Rosa's eyes practically asked her to share. "But I am kind of stressed today. You were right about that. And it actually does have to do with my son," she said as the rest of the residents drifted away.

"Has he gotten worse?"

"I'm not sure. He's been getting low a lot, which means his blood sugar's been taking nosedives. I just found out that he's going to have to go back to the hospital for another round of tests," she said slowly. "But I'll play on Monday. Kay should be fine with that." Though it was a school holiday for Hank, she hadn't even thought about asking for the day off.

For a moment, Rosa's eyes softened. "That's fine, Susan. We'll see each other on Monday. No problem."

"Thanks for understanding."

"Mind if I give you a piece of advice?"

She shook her head.

"You put that boy of yours first, every single day. A mother's duty is more important than any job."

"I know that. But it doesn't pay the bills."

"Bills will get paid—they always do, sooner or later. But you can't get days missed back. I can promise you that."

Susan would have hugged the lady if she was the kind of person who hugged. "Thanks, Mrs. Ventura."

The older woman waved Susan off with a hand. "We don't need a scene now. Now, you best go mill around and chat with the rest of the folks here. The last thing you need is the dragon lady to fuss at you again."

Doing her best not to chuckle at the name, Susan stood up. "Thanks, I will."

"And, Susan?"

"Yes, ma'am?"

"That Stan is sitting over there by himself, struggling with his crossword again. Why don't you go see if he needs some help. He almost always does. He's not too smart, you know."

"I'll go do that right now."

ON SATURDAY AFTERNOON, Cal was sipping a Coke from the machine and trying to determine how many cattle they should plan to take to market, when two people he hoped never to see again in his lifetime appeared down the hall. The smaller of the pair scampered over.

"Hi, Mr. Riddell. It's me, Hank."

Seeing them only made him recall being a complete and total jackass. Holding out his hand, he shook Hank's. "Hey, buddy. How are y'all doing?"

"Not so good," Hank said as his mother approached and stood right behind him. "We're here. Again."

Susan patted her son's shoulder. "It couldn't be helped."

"In that case, I'm sorry to see you." When her eyes narrowed, he silently groaned. Was he ever going to be able to have a conversation with her without sticking his foot in the middle of it? "What I meant to say was, I thought this place would have been just a memory for y'all by now."

Hank answered for the still-silent Susan. "Well…we were home, but now we're back. I'm getting tests again, aren't I, Mom?"

"Tests?" A strange sensation burned the back of his neck, reminding him that he hadn't spared a thought about why Hank was getting stuck so much.

"Yes. More tests." Susan nodded, punctuating the gesture with a smile that didn't come close to meeting her eyes. "Excuse us. We need to be on our way, as well."

Now he felt even lower than a snake's belly. Just because he was in a permanent bad mood, it didn't mean he had to take it out on innocent women and children. "About the other day—I'm sorry if I was a bit abrupt."

"A bit?"

"A lot. This thing with my dad, it's brought out the worst in me. I'm sorry," he repeated. "And, Hank, you're right. I shouldn't have said shut up to you."

Hank grinned, showing a wide gap where an incisor used to be. "S'okay."

For a moment, he didn't think she was going to respond. Then, ever so slowly, she nodded. "Apology accepted. Now, we really need to be on our way."

Just as she passed, Cal smelled gardenias again. Gardenias and something spicy underneath. For too long, his gaze tarried on that auburn hair of hers, wondering how a person could manage so much of it...when he met the boy's eyes.

"Hank, are you ready?" a nurse asked as he approached.

"Sure." Hank grimaced. "Sorry, but I've gotta go. I've got to go pee in a cup."

"Good luck with that."

Hank grinned. "Thanks," he said as the nurse escorted him down the hall. "See ya, Mom."

"Okay." She smiled at him and the nurse until they were out of sight. Only then did the full extent of her worries cross her face.

Making Cal feel another tug toward her. As he knew

from his experience with his little sister, Ginny, nothing was harder than worrying about the health of a child. "Well, ma'am. You take care now, Susan," he said, nodding as he stepped away.

"Wait." She swallowed. "I forgot to ask. How's your father?"

"Truth is, I don't know. His double bypass ended up being a triple and, as you can imagine, he's having quite a time."

"I'm so sorry about that."

"Thank you." Unbidden, a lump formed in his throat. His father's operation had felt never ending. And he'd looked so pale and lifeless in the recovery room, tears had formed in Cal's eyes. Now he was waiting for more information, but he was having to wait and wait for answers—something that rarely happened in his life. Usually the Riddell name got things done.

"How old is he?"

"Sixty-two."

"Ah."

"Yeah. Too young for the condition his heart was in, I'm afraid. And, of course, he's not afraid to complain loudly and, uh, colorfully. The air's pretty blue."

Again she surprised him by laughing. "I work at the Electra Lodge, so I know all about ornery senior citizens. By the time folks get to be a certain age, they seem to have decided that watching their tongue is overrated."

Her words surprised a chuckle. "They might be right about that. My dad now says whatever's on his mind. No filters. It's all I can do to shield my poor sister's ears."

"Sister?"

"Ginny. She's only six." When she blinked in surprise, Cal decided to do some explaining. "My father, he was remarried for a time."

"Oh, my."

"Yeah, we were shocked to silence when she came along, too." They'd been really shocked when Ginny's mother, Carolyn, decided to take off without a backward glance.

Again, pain from the past threatened to reach out and strangle him. Seeing his dad so sick reminded him of his mother getting cancer. Thinking about his sister spurred a memory of their father trying to explain to him and his brothers why his new wife had left.

He cleared his throat. "I better get going. If my dad's awake, he's likely to be causing some poor nurse to blush. Saying he cusses like a sailor is pretty much an understatement."

Susan murmured, "Don't be too tough on him. Bodies don't recover easily at that age."

"I guess you see that a lot at work?"

"Uh-huh. It's not just a retirement home, you know. The full name of the place is Electra Lodge and Rehabilitation Center."

She sounded like an advertisement. "I've driven by it. It, uh, looks like a nice place." He'd passed by the redbrick building often but had never gone in. "Is it?"

"I think so. Though, I'm kind of new."

"Ah." As he eyed her full lips again, Cal knew something bad was happening to him. He was starting to think about her as a woman instead of someone really irritating.

He wasn't pleased.

Fact was, he couldn't recall ever meeting another woman who'd gotten him so hot and bothered so fast. Well, not since Christy—and he'd thought no one would piss him off the way she could. Just the memory of her deceitfulness created a hurt in his belly that no amount of Rolaids could ever cure.

And now Susan was making him feel that same odd combination of irritation and desire.

He didn't appreciate it. He had a million other things on his mind, the most important of which was lying in one of the rooms on the third floor.

So how come he'd been finding ways to sneak glances at the way her hips curved out in a completely feminine, pleasing way? How come he was noticing the way the ivory skin of her neck contrasted so well with the dark auburn hair floating halfway down her back? How come he was kind of hoping she'd smile again his way?

He scrambled for something to say. "So…are you planning to stay here for a while?"

"I hope so. I just got the job."

"No. I mean here at the hospital."

"Here? Oh, no. We really need to get a handle on this diabetes stuff so I can get back to work."

"Diabetes?" Cal struggled to recall what he knew about the disease, to show that he wasn't completely self-centered. "Isn't your boy kind of young for that?"

"It's type 1. You know, juvenile diabetes." When he couldn't help but stare at her blankly, she added, "It does hit *juveniles,* you know. He's young enough for that."

Cal tried to recall some article he'd read in the dentist's waiting room. "Don't you get diabetes from a poor diet or something? You know, you probably shouldn't be letting him eat hot dogs."

In an instant, all traces of friendliness vanished. Pure loathing lashed out at him. "For your information, Mr. Riddell, type 1 diabetes is an autoimmune disease. You can't 'get it' from hot dogs."

Crap. "Oh. I'm—"

"What? You're a genius at diseases because you're standing in a hospital?" she interrupted. "You know what?

I think I liked you better when you stuck to one-word answers."

Cal almost tried to explain himself again, but he felt like a fool. And he really hated feeling like a fool.

Instead, he opted for just standing there as she sashayed down the hall, pushed the elevator button and waited for the doors to open.

And waited.

As she stood and fumed—and as he watched her fume—Cal knew he should do something. The right thing to do would be to go up to her and apologize. Again. No woman wanted to hear anything bad about her mothering skills.

But memories of getting burned ran deep. Long ago, Christy had made such a laughingstock out of him that he'd quit the rodeo circuit.

For months, all everyone and their brother talked about was how he'd been whipped well and good by a tiny gal from Texarkana.

So self-preservation kicked in. The better thing to do was to keep himself still. Distant. Then he wouldn't get hurt.

He didn't move a muscle until those elevator doors closed behind her.

Chapter Three

Hours later, back at the ranch, all hell was breaking loose.

"Cal, where've you been?" Ginny cried the moment he walked in through the front door, her face streaked with tears and chocolate.

He grunted as she strung two arms around him, getting his starched shirt smeared with streaks of brown goo. Slowly, he wrapped his arms around her, giving in to the inevitable. "I've been at the hospital helping Dad," he said soothingly. "You know that."

"I tr-tried to call you. You didn't pick up."

He patted her some more. "That's 'cause you've got to turn off your cell phones in the hospital. What's wrong? Did you get in a fight again?" His scrappy sister couldn't seem to regulate her temper. Time and again, in true Riddell fashion, she let her emotions get the best of her, much to her teacher's dismay.

"No." She dug in her head, plastering her cheek against his belly. As always, a deep, all-encompassing love filled him for the girl. His little slip of a sister.

"So what's got you so riled up?" he murmured, patting her long brown hair. Hair the same shade as his own.

Raising his head, he was relieved to see Gwen standing in the hall leading to the kitchen. Gwen was a grandmother whose grandchildren lived in Houston. She'd missed living with a family, and they'd all needed a woman's hand in helping raise Virginia after Carolyn had taken off. In return for room and board, Gwen helped out as much as she could.

Her lips pursed when their eyes met.

"What's going on?" he mouthed.

"A lot." She sighed. "We got a call about an hour ago. Trent's in the hospital in Albuquerque."

He stiffened. "What? When?"

Ginny untangled herself from his arms and pulled him down to eye level. "A bull threw him and he hurt his ribs. Bad. And his arm and a kidney, too." Eyes wide, she said, "Right, Gwen?"

"Kind of." Her lips curved slightly. "His arm is broken. And the rest of him isn't so good."

Cal felt his insides do a flip turn. Of the three brothers, Trent was by far the most talented bull rider. His younger brother was fearless in the ring, and had enough confidence for the whole family.

He'd won so many buckles and trophies that the rest of them just kind of counted on him always coming out of the pen the winner. So much so that Cal had begun to take his brother's performances almost for granted. Sometimes, he even forgot to look at the recaps on the computer or check in with Trent on a regular basis.

But now Cal realized he'd been foolish to imagine that his brother was invincible. "How bad is not good?" he asked around a sinking feeling of dread. "Do I need to go fly out there?"

"I don't think so. From what I can gather, in addition to the broken arm, two ribs are cracked." Lowering her voice, she added, "He might have a concussion, too. They're doing tests today to check for any internal injuries."

"But that's all?" he asked sarcastically.

"It could be worse," Gwen murmured, her brown eyes sympathetic. "No one thinks there's anything life threatening. He's going to be checked out momentarily. We'll just have to wait and see."

Wait and see. First for his dad, now for his brother. Cal didn't reckon he had too much patience left inside him. "I, for one, am getting pretty tired of doing that wait-and-see two-step. It's wearin' me out."

"I feel the same way," she said with a commiserating look. "Just so you know, I called Jarred in Mexico."

"I'm glad you did. What did he say?"

"Nothing, because he didn't pick up. I must have called four times, too. He didn't pick up that phone once."

"You'd think the boy could manage to check messages every once in a while. No one can be in bed that much."

Gwen winced. "Honestly, Junior. Watch your tongue."

Ginny scrambled out of his arms. "How come Jarred's in bed? Is he sick, too?"

"Just lovesick." When his sister's eyes widened, Cal rushed to give her another answer. "I mean, he's fine. Now, don't you be worrying about Jarred. I was only joking, sweetheart."

Her lips trembled. "Okay."

When he spied a tear slide down her face, mixing in with her chocolate mess, he reached out for her again. "Ginny, I just told you the God's honest truth. How come you're crying again?"

"I want everyone to come on home and be like it used to be."

"That would be nice." He'd like that, too. But even in a month of Sundays, it sure as hell wasn't going to happen. Things had happened. Their dad got old and he and his brothers grew up.

"When's Daddy coming home?"

"Now, that's something I'm not sure about." Leading Ginny into the kitchen, he pulled out her white step stool. "Hop up," he ordered. Then returning to the conversation about their dad, he said, "Here's the thing. Dad's going to need a lot of special help."

"How much?"

"A lot. He's not going to be able to do a lot of things by himself, and he's going to need round-the-clock care, too." Looking Gwen's way, he said, "That's going to mean lots of driving and sitting around. And sitting and watching. Any chance you could help out with that?"

Gwen frowned. "Junior, I like you enough to even sit by your father's side and get chewed on regularly. But I just don't think I can."

"You don't?" His heart sank.

Tilting her head in Ginny's direction, she said, "I could help out some, of course, but really I don't think I'll have that kind of time. Someone's got to get this little thing where she needs to go...." Her voice drifted off. Obviously Gwen was uncomfortable telling him no.

But she had a valid point. Ginny needed her regular routine. Disruptions meant outbursts and fights in school and tears at home...and that wasn't going to be good for anyone.

"You're right. I know. We've got a lot going on...." He turned on the faucet, picked up the hand soap and held it up. "Hands."

Dutifully, Ginny stuck them out. He squirted. "Rub. Now rinse."

As she did as he requested, he pulled over a couple of paper towels and dampened them, then did a cursory scrub over her cheeks. That was what life was all about with a six-year-old girl, he supposed.

Drama and dirt.

As soon as she was clean and dry, he sat with her and Gwen at the kitchen table. "I just don't know how we're going to give him the care he needs."

"What are you thinking?"

"I was thinking we'd just care for him here…but now with Trent in the hospital, too, I don't think that's going to fly."

"Maybe a rehabilitation place?" She snapped her fingers. "There's the Electra Lodge."

Reluctantly he nodded. "The hospital recommended that, as a matter of fact. I guess Dad could stay there for a month and get the round-the-clock attention he deserves."

Gwen perked up. "What's it like? Have you heard?"

"It's probably pretty nice. We could check it out.…" But all Cal could think about was the fact that Susan Young worked there. It would sure be his just deserts if his dad ended up being cared for by Susan. Every visit there was sure to be filled with irritation and arguments.

If they were even that lucky.

"Daddy's gonna want to be home with me," Ginny interjected.

"I know he's going to want to be home with you, sugar. But we don't have too much of a choice. Dad has health issues," he said vaguely. "And other issues, too."

"When he gets better, he'll be able to ride all the time."

"I hope so."

Looking at him directly, Gwen asked, "So do we have a plan?"

"I'm afraid so. I'll try to contact Jarred and Trent, but unless they want to play nursemaid, it's the best solution. He's going to need more care than we can give him. Plus, he's gonna be as cranky as all get-out, too. You know he's going to take exception to anything I say. He always does. We don't have time for that."

"Good luck with that conversation."

"Thanks. I'm going to need it."

Ginny tugged on his shirt. "Cal? Are you mad now?"

"Not at all, sugar." Forcing a grin, he bent down to her. "What do you say we go check on the horses? Maybe they'd like a little snack."

As he'd expected, she hopped from her stool and grinned. "I bet Casper wants an apple."

"I'm sure that horse does. Pick one out and I'll cut it up, sugar."

"Do you think we'll ever get a better TV?" Hank asked as Susan tried once again to get the salt-and-pepper mess off the nineteen-inch screen in their tiny living room.

"I do," she replied. She was absolutely positive they would get a better television. *One day.*

Hank narrowed his eyes. "Soon?"

"No."

Hank sighed. "Jeremy has a television in his room that's bigger than this. You wouldn't believe how good it looks."

"Oh, I would. This TV isn't too big at all. But we've got other things to pay for, Hank. It can't be helped."

"Maybe we could do without some things. Then we'd have more money for the good stuff."

"What are you thinking we could do without?" She, for one, didn't have a plan. Already her car was limping along and her clothes were mainly purchased from resale shops.

"I don't know. Broccoli?"

"Broccoli's not making as much of a dent in our budget as you might think, buddy."

He slumped. "I guess you're right." He looked down at his shoes. "Guess I can't buy new sneakers, huh?"

Little by little, her heart broke. She hated not being able

to get him the things he wanted. "Maybe we can get new shoes after I get paid."

He flashed a smile. "'Kay." Walking away, he opened up the fridge. "So, can I have an apple?"

Once upon a time, the answer to that question would have been automatic. But now she hesitated. There were sugar levels and dietary concerns she couldn't afford to ignore. "What else have you eaten today?"

After he told her, she mentally reviewed the dietary guidelines that the nurses had given her. "I suppose so. But let me know if you start to feel funny."

Hank rolled his eyes as he bit into an apple, then scooted toward the tiny TV and watched his regular series of shows on the Cartoon Network.

Usually, this would be the time that Susan would lean back and stretch and relax. But all she could do was watch Hank watch TV and worry.

She'd gotten the lab results. They were going to need to up Hank's insulin dose. And though the nurse probably didn't mean to sound like it, Susan had the uncomfortable feeling that the nurse thought she wasn't monitoring his levels closely enough.

After scheduling yet another appointment with the pediatrician, Susan had hung up…and had wondered how in the world she would manage to get off even more time from work. Kay was going to be put out, that was for sure.

And how was she going to be able to start monitoring things better with Hank? When they weren't going to all these doctor's appointments, she'd be spending even less time with him, not more.

"I'm going to sit on the patio," she told Hank, then walked out to her nine-by-nine concrete slab and took a seat.

The moment she closed her eyes, the furnace that was

Texas in September engulfed her. On cue, she started to sweat. Any sane person would go on into the air-conditioning. But maybe that was the problem. She wasn't sane. Not by a long shot.

Why else would she have left Children's Hospital in Cincinnati, and all her family…for Electra, Texas?

Maybe she should go back to Cincinnati. Living in the city would be difficult and more expensive, but she could probably find a good job. And then Hank would have everything he needed in case something went wrong.…

"You in for the night, Susan?" Betsy, her neighbor, peeked out in between the row of holly bushes that separated their patios.

"I am. What about you?"

The closest friend she had in Electra smiled a gap-toothed grin. "Not on your life! It's only seven o'clock."

Once upon a time, Susan had thought that way, too. Now, though, seven meant she could finally sit down and relax. "Hey, want to come over for a minute?"

"Of course. Let me get a pair of Buds and I'll be right there."

Minutes later, Betsy arrived, her hands full of Bud Lights and a spunky sashay in her walk. "Hot enough for you?" she asked as she flopped down on Susan's extra lawn chair. As she did so, the hem of her cotton sundress fluttered around her thighs.

"More than enough. I don't know when I'm ever going to get used to it being ninety in September."

"Give it a few dozen years. Then it will seem as normal as dust storms in July."

"In the meantime, I'll just pray for good air-conditioning." As they shared a chuckle, Susan sipped her beer, then looked her girlfriend over. Betsy was an office manager for a cellular-phone company and one of five siblings who all lived around the area. She always had something going on, either with work or with her family. "So, how are you? How was your day?"

"Irritating. Too many people were wanting things I can't give them." Running a hand through her short, spiky hair, she sighed. "But that's okay. It's Labor Day weekend and I've managed to get two out of the next three days off. Hey, want to come to a party with me tonight?"

"Thanks, but I can't. I've got Hank."

"We need to find you a sitter, Susan. You can't spend every Friday night home."

Until the doctors got Hank's body under control, Susan didn't want to risk Hank being in a sitter's care more than she had to. And right now, he was already going to have to be with a sitter for most of Monday.

And, well, being home on a Friday night wasn't that much of a tragedy for her. She liked the peace and quiet.

For the most part. "Where's the party?" she asked, mainly to get Betsy's focus off her.

"At Buffalo Bob's. Do you know it?"

"Nope. But it's got a catchy name."

"It's a play on Buffalo Bill, you know," Betsy said earnestly. "Anyway, Bob's is a honky-tonk down the way." Betsy's eyes lit up as if it was her birthday. "Every Labor Day, they put on a big ol' party. A real celebration. I'm telling you what, it's a good time. Susan, there's even gonna be fireworks!"

"Sounds like fun."

"It's a hoot, that's what it is. Lots of people will be there. You're missing out."

"I know." It did sound fun. She used to look forward to Friday nights like no other. There was something to be said for kicking up her heels and letting off steam, and she'd done her fair share of that.

Well, she had until she'd become a mother. Now, sipping a glass of wine with her feet up and a good book sounded like heaven. With maybe a man rubbing her shoulders, too. Maybe even rubbing other places, too, she mused, her mouth going dry.

Gosh, how long had it been since she'd been on the receiving end of a man's tender touch?

Still chatting about the bar, Betsy threw back the rest of her beer, then added, "Susan, it's gonna be such a party. I heard even Cal Riddell might show up."

Susan almost choked on her beer. "You're kidding."

"I'm not." Betsy set down her Bud. "Wait a minute. You're acting like you know something I don't. Do you actually know Cal Riddell?"

"Yes." Though she sure wished she didn't.

Betsy's golden eyes lit up. "Oh, honey. That's awesome! Isn't he gorgeous?"

He…was. But that didn't really matter.

"Are you friends with him?"

"Not so much."

Lowering her voice, Betsy leaned forward. "To tell you the truth, I tried to be more than friends with his brother a few months ago, but he blew me off."

"Brother?"

"Trent. He's a legit rodeo star."

"Wow. I didn't know that."

"So, don't you think that Cal Riddell is something else?"

It was a struggle to not offer her opinion. "He was something, all right."

"My goodness, but he's a fine looking man. Six foot three, black hair, blue-gray eyes…" Betsy fanned the air for emphasis. "And the way he talks. I swear, his voice is so deep. And that slow drawl, it's enough to curl your toes."

Susan had noticed that drawl.

"And, well, he's rich as sin, too."

Though she was telling herself she couldn't care less about that man, Susan couldn't help but catch hold of Betsy's latest tidbit. "He's rich?"

"Hell, yes! And we're not talking rich like he-can-take-a-vacation-whenever-he-wants rich. We're talking rich enough to-buy-himself-a-plane-and-pilot rich." After a pause, Betsy said softly, "He's rich enough to support a wife in the way she'd like to be accustomed to."

Though she was vaguely disturbed by Betsy's words, Susan elected to ignore them. "Hmm," she said simply. "I really had no idea."

"You still don't. Sue, he's *Cal Riddell,* as in the *Riddell Ranch.*"

Betsy said that as if he was a celebrity or something. Well, she, for one, had never heard of the Riddells or their infamous ranch.

Come to think of it, she wouldn't shed a tear if she never heard of the place again. Choosing her words carefully, Susan said, "Actually…I wasn't all that impressed with him."

"Get out."

"I'm serious. We shared a table in the cafeteria at the hospital when Hank was getting tests done. The whole time, rich Cal Riddell couldn't have been ruder."

"That's not like him. Usually, he hardly ever talks. It's part of his charm, you know."

Susan wished he'd been a little more quietly charming. Though… "He was a little nicer when our paths crossed at the hospital today."

"See?"

"He was nice until he insulted me."

"Uh-oh."

Though Susan realized she was ranting, she just kept on going. "Uh-oh is right. He's the biggest jerk alive. I hope I never see him again."

"You ought to get those eyes of yours cleaned. He's a catch and a half."

"Not for me. I certainly don't want to catch him. I just want to stay out of his way."

"I bet you'll feel differently about him once y'all dance. I'd feel all kinds of things for him if I pressed up against him real close."

Susan couldn't imagine the man she'd met unbend enough to dance at all. She couldn't even imagine trying to have a conversation with him in a bar! Nor did she ever want to try.

So, if she couldn't imagine any of that...why could she definitely imagine what it would feel like to be pressed up close to him?

She cleared her throat. "Unfortunately, I won't be dancing with anyone tonight. But you be sure and tell me how the party is."

Betsy looked her over and frowned. "Susan, you need to put yourself out there if you want to meet anyone."

"I know. And I have been meeting people. I've met a lot of people at work, you know."

"Doctors and old people don't count."

Before Susan could dispute that, Betsy picked up her empty bottle and stood. "Well, I need to go shower and get cute." Shaking her spiky red hair, she grinned. "This magic don't happen on its own, you know."

"Have fun, Betsy."

With a little wave, her friend turned and disappeared through the hedge.

And left Susan thinking about a long Friday night with nothing to do but sit and stew. And to wonder what it would be like to actually have money to spend on clubs and parties.

And to wonder how her life might have been different if Hank's dad had decided to stay.

Chapter Four

Sunday brought church and another hospital visit. As Cal held Ginny's hand while she skipped down the hall, he prayed again for patience.

Praying for patience was pretty much a constant thing now, though he wasn't sure if anyone was actually listening to him. Lately, all he seemed to be doing was biting his tongue while everyone else gave him grief.

Or told him their troubles. Or asked for more than he could give. Frankly, Cal had a feeling all his tolerance for the year had been used up sometime during the second week of January. From that point on, he'd been living on borrowed time.

"We're almost there, Junior," Ginny announced, skipping along by his side on her tippy-toes. "We're almost at Daddy's door."

"Uh-huh."

"When I see him, I'm going to give him a big hug."

"You know you can't do that," he warned. "He's had surgery, remember?"

"But you said he was better!"

"His heart is, not his mood." As Ginny struggled to digest that tidbit, Cal directed her over to the side of the hallway and knelt down on one knee. The last thing in the world he wanted was for Ginny to get her feelings hurt.

And because their dad was in no condition to watch his mouth, Cal figured his little sister should be prepared for the worst. "Ginny, honey, I just want to warn you that Dad's been in a bear of a mood. So, he might not be super happy to see us. You know what I mean?"

"No. He's always happy to see me."

She had a point there. If anyone could make the old man be almost companionable, it was his little sister. "He will be happy to see you, but he might forget to act like it." Or tell her, Cal added grimly. Actually, that was probably putting it kindly. In the years since Cal's mother passed away, his father had gradually lost whatever town polish he'd slapped on when he got rich and spent time in Dallas.

With every passing month, Cal Sr. seemed to care less about offending people and more about saying what was on his mind.

And there was always a lot on Dad's mind. Nowadays, he didn't watch his tongue in the best of situations. And when Dad was really in a mood, well, all bets were off that anything kind and sweet would pass through his lips.

Chances were good that this was one of those days.

When they started walking again, Ginny slipped her hand in Cal's. "Junior?" she said with a tug.

"Hmm?"

"You're frowning. Aren't you happy to see me, too?"

Taking a knee again, he pulled her into a tight hug. "I'm always happy to see you. Always."

She wrapped her skinny arms around his neck and pressed her cheek against his neck, the way she always did. "And Jarred and Trent, too?"

"Of course. Sugar, Dad loves you, too. He's just a grump sometimes."

"A grumpy Gus."

"Yep. Okay now, let's go see how he's doing," he murmured when they finally got to their dad's door.

Slowly twisting the handle, he peeked in. "Dad?"

Lying on the bed, looking beat-up and pissed off, Calvin Sr. glared his way. "I'm here. Where else would I be?"

Cal matched his father's glare with one of his own. "Ginny's here with me. She wanted to come see you." Cal made sure he put the emphasis on *she,* just so his dad would know that Cal's patience was up and gone.

Before he could give his father any additional warning glances, Ginny broke free from his hand and scampered in. "Hey, Daddy!" she hollered. Surely loud enough to wake the patients down the hall.

Quickly Cal reached for her but was too late. "Gin—" he warned. "Watch—"

She either didn't hear or didn't care to abide his warning, because she was flying toward the bed like a bullet.

Ready to jump and cause a heap of trouble....

"Stop!" Calvin called out, his face full of alarm.

Ginny skidded to a stop. "Daddy?"

"You settle down, girl. You're in the hospital, not the circus. You hear me?"

"Yes, sir," she said meekly, then turned Cal's way.

As he saw her bottom lip begin to quiver, he took two steps forward and reached for her hand again. "Remember how I said Daddy's had surgery?" he murmured as their father continued to scowl. "You've got to move a whole lot slower in here. You could have hurt him."

Turning back to their dad, Ginny started moving in slow motion. "Is this better, Daddy?"

She looked ridiculous. But instead of smiling Ginny's way, their dad glowered at him. "Why did you bring her?"

Ginny stopped again. Cal placed a reassuring hand on

her shoulder. "I brought her because she wanted to see you. Though, with the way you're acting, I don't know why."

Twin spots of color appeared on their father's cheeks.

When they were stopped in front of his bed, Ginny let go of Cal's hand and placed both of hers on the bars surrounding the hospital bed. "You don't look good, Daddy."

"Thanks. I don't feel good."

"Cal says you're grumpy 'cause you don't like people messing with your heart, on account it don't work too well. What was wrong with the old one?"

"I smoked and ate too much."

Ginny paused a bit, digesting that bit of news. Then she rose on her tiptoes and stared at his chest. "Do you have a scar?"

"I do."

"Is it big?"

"It is."

She leaned forward, turning her head slightly so her eye was peeking out through the bars on the side of the bed. "Can I see it?"

"No."

"Why not?"

Slowly, their father raised his eyes to Cal's and sighed. "You can't see it because it's all bandaged up."

"But you'll be all better soon?"

To Cal's relief, their father chuckled. "I think so, darlin'."

After a moment, Ginny rearranged herself in front of the metal bars again. Now, as she peered at her daddy through the openings, Cal imagined she looked like a prisoner in a jail cell. "So, are you happy to see me now?"

Cal held his breath. There was no telling what his dad was going to say to that. His father was in extreme pain, and possibly loopy from medication, too. Mentally, he cursed himself. He should have known better than to bring his little sister in. All this was going to do was aggravate their father and cause Ginny unnecessary grief.

And then he, of course, was going to have to deal with it.

But then, in the blink of an eye, Cal watched his father's whole disposition change yet again. Gone was the pissed-off expression, the frown between his salt-and-pepper brows. In its place was the kind of sweet, special smile Cal only saw when his father worked with his prized gelding, Vixen, or talked with Ginny. "Of course I am. You never fail to brighten my day." Reaching out, he tapped her knuckles. "Whatcha been doing? Have you been a good girl?"

"I've been helping Cal around the house. I've been helping Gwen, too. We made Rice Krispie treats." She swiveled her head and looked up at him. "I've been real good, right?"

Cal nodded slowly. "Pretty good."

"How many fights?"

Ginny stuck up her finger. "Only one this week, and the playground aide didn't even look that upset about it."

Cal pressed his hands on Ginny's shoulders. "Ginny's only gotten four time-outs this week, too."

Their dad's eyes lit right up in amusement, though Cal could see he was trying hard to be serious. "Virginia Ann, you're more trouble than all three of your brothers combined! What am I ever going to do with you?"

She looked down at her feet. "I don't know."

"Come now. What do I always say?"

Slowly, she looked up at her dad. "Love me a lot?"

Calvin's smiled widened, but Cal noticed that it also looked strained. "That's a fact. When I get home, we'll have to watch TV together."

"Okay. *The Biggest Loser*'s on again." She and her daddy were reality-show junkies.

"What about *Survivor?*"

"I'm not sure. Cal hasn't let me watch it since that man took off all his clothes and that boy and girl started kissing in the dark."

"It really wasn't appropriate for a six-year-old, Dad."

"Good TV, though," his dad remarked. "But, uh, probably not so good for little girls. Your brother's just lookin' out for you."

"But you'll watch TV with me soon?"

"Of course, sweetheart. It's a date."

Ginny leaned closer, eyeing the IV tube. "Does that hurt?"

"Nah."

"Just your heart?"

"Just my heart. And my ribs."

"Poor Daddy." Ever so slowly, one by one, her fingers loosened on the bed rail and she thrust her hand through. "I've missed you."

"I've missed my little girl, too." He reached out a hand. "Come here, pumpkin. Come hold my hand for a sec."

She did as he asked, her tentative expression morphing into a full-blown grin as she stepped closer.

Cal took the empty seat and let the two of them have their time together. In a way that he'd never done with his boys, Calvin Sr. asked Ginny a dozen questions and listened intently to each answer. Within five minutes, he'd heard all about school and her dolls and even got an update on Spot—the puppy Jarred's girlfriend, Serena, had brought home. "You're not letting that dog chew up my slippers, are you?"

Ginny's little mouth formed a circle. "Oh, no, sir."

"That's good." He yawned. "I'm getting tired now and

you need to get out of this hospital. There's sick people everywhere. Before you know it, they're going to make you sick, too. Now, is your brother going to take you to lunch? Because I think visiting folks here should at least earn you a meal."

Cal stood up. "I am. We're going to go get shakes and burgers at the Sonic, aren't we?"

"And go to Shop-N-Go. Cal said maybe I could get some new crayons."

"If you do, will you draw me a picture?"

Ginny's face lit up as if her daddy had just given her the sun and the moon. "Uh-huh. I'll bring it next time."

"I'll look forward to it."

Their dad looked to be fading fast, so Cal cleared his throat. "It's time, sugar."

"Bye, baby," Dad said.

Ginny blew him a kiss, then trotted back over to Cal. "I'm ready now." She peeked out the door, then turned back to Cal. "The nurses' station has suckers. Can I go get me one?"

"You may."

When they were alone, his dad looked like the grumpy old man that he was once again. With a ragged sigh, he leaned back into the pillows and closed his eyes. "That girl. She's everything and a day, ain't she?"

Cal smiled. "Yes, sir."

"Really only four time-outs?"

"That's all I've heard from her teacher." Cal shrugged. "'Course, the year's just starting. Ginny might be starting off slow. You know…breaking her teacher in slowly."

His dad looked as if he was trying to look perturbed, but his eyes were glowing. "Maybe I should've told her no more often."

"I tell her no all the time. It doesn't seem to do much good."

"Perhaps you've got a point."

"Dad, do you need anything?"

"Only the same things as ever. I need to get pain free and out of here. I'm ready to go home."

Except, he wasn't going to be able to go home anytime soon.

But because he wasn't ready to bring that up, Cal concentrated on his dad's pain. "Want me to call for the nurse?"

"Nah, I'll push my button when y'all leave." After a moment, he murmured, "I'm glad you brought our girl here, son. Thank you."

"You're welcome. She loves you." Briefly, Cal wondered why it was so easy to talk about Ginny's love but not his own. Now was the time to tell him about Trent, but the words stuck in his throat. "So, Dad, we got a phone call...."

"What happened? Was it the accountant?"

"No. Business wise, everything's fine." Cal paused. "It's about Trent. Dad, Trent got hurt in Albuquerque."

"Oh, I know that," he said wearily. "I wondered if you were ever going to tell me about it, though."

"I didn't want to bother you about it."

"I'm old and falling apart, but I'm still your father. Trent knows that. He called last night. I talked to him." He shook his head. "That boy's going to be the death of me. If that little girl of ours doesn't wear me out first."

"I spoke with his doctor. He's going to be okay. Just out of commission."

"Hope he'll use the time to come home for a while. I asked him to."

"He said he'll probably get this way in a month or so."

"A month, huh? That boy. Always doing what he's wanted to."

Privately, Cal agreed. Sometimes, Cal felt Trent's independence was a slap in the face. All his life Cal had done what was expected of him, and had gotten very little in the way of recognition for it. Trent, on the other hand, had made a small fortune in the saddle…and most times acted as if that was enough for any man.

Cal frowned as his dad shifted again. "So, you're feeling better?"

"Hell, no. My whole body hurts like the devil. Plus, every time I turn around, a nurse comes in and wants to poke and prod me."

"Junior?" Ginny said from the door.

"I'm still here, Gin."

"You coming?"

"In a minute. Now sit for a sec."

"Take care of your sister," his dad muttered. "She's waiting on you."

"I'll be right there. But she can cool her heels for a while, too."

"It's doubtful."

"One day she'll learn some patience. Maybe."

Slowly, a new awareness filled his dad's gaze. Pride. And maybe, understanding? "You're a good son, Junior," he said after a bit. "If I haven't told you lately, I want you to know I'm proud of you," he said gruffly. "You do a good job with Ginny."

With that, he turned his head away and closed his eyes.

Cal knew better than to reach out and touch his dad. But still, he felt that brush of acceptance as strong as if his father had gripped him in a bear hug. "I'll be back this evening."

"Not necessary."

"Don't worry. I won't stay for long."

As his father grumbled, Cal directed Ginny out before he could say anything more. Once they were halfway down the hallway, he said, "Gin, what do you say we go eat some cheeseburgers?"

"Can I have a shake, too?"

"Always," he said, taking her hand. As once again she skipped down the hallway by his side.

SUSAN'S WORK SCHEDULE wasn't getting any easier. If anything, it seemed to double every week. Though Susan knew some of that stemmed from being new and unused to some computer procedures, some of the fault was of her own making, too. Time and again she'd feel her mind drift, and she'd start thinking about Hank and his unhappiness about Electra. Next thing she knew, the guilt she'd felt for moving him from his friends and family would settle in, hard.

No, the only thing that had sparked happiness in her son was Mr. Riddell—much to her dismay.

Cal Riddell. No matter how much she tried to erase him from her thoughts, he seemed to turn up like that bad penny. First there was Hank talking about him. And then Betsy mentioning him.

And now, every few minutes, she kept finding her mind running his way. In spite of her best efforts, Susan kept thinking about his blue-gray eyes and his perpetually serious expression. And the way he sneaked glances her way... even the way he sparred with her about everything and nothing.

She couldn't recall the last person who seemed to take such pleasure in getting her back up.

Susan was sitting at her computer screen, wondering what, exactly, he did all day at his ranch, when—just her luck—Paula appeared at her doorway and announced his arrival.

Susan snapped her head up. "What was that?"

"Oh, you heard me correctly," Paula said with a cheeky smile. Lowering her voice, she added, "He said he wouldn't see anybody but you."

Right there and then, the temperature of her body rose a good ten degrees. She'd just stood up when he appeared at her doorway, looking like her girlish dreams of the Marlboro Man—white felt Stetson, pale gray dress shirt, dark denims, silver buckle.

Gorgeous.

"Ms. Young," he said, tipping his hat slightly. "Cal Riddell."

Really? He'd really introduced himself again? As if she wouldn't have recognized him? Her mouth went dry. "How nice to see you again," she said. Calmly. Professionally. Inside, though, she felt her nerves kick into high gear. "Please, have a seat." She gestured to one of the chairs across from her desk.

"Ma'am?"

Belatedly, she realized he was waiting for her to take a chair first. "Oh." She took the chair next to him, but forgot to straighten her skirt as she did so, so it lay crooked across her thighs. A little too high on her left.

In a fluid move, he sat down, his gaze straying across her legs before he looked directly at her face.

"What can I help you with?"

It took him a few seconds to answer, as though he was getting his thoughts together but having a difficult time doing it. Finally, he murmured, "Do you remember me talking about my dad? About how he just had heart surgery?"

"Of course." She remembered that…and a whole bunch of other things about him. "How is he doing?"

A light flickered in those amazing eyes of his. "Grumpy as all get-out."

"Obviously, heart surgery is tough on a person's body—"

He cut her off. "The doctors said he's going to need some extra help for quite a bit. At least a month."

"I see."

"I remembered you talking about this place." He shifted, then looked around her office as if he was expecting more than the plain, utilitarian space that it was. "You made it seem nice."

Susan bit her lip. Was he being ironic? "I think it is nice."

A muscle in his cheek jumped. "Think y'all can take him in?"

The look in his eyes was dark and cool and…full of longing. As though he'd give anything if she'd just help him out.

Something inside her turned all languid and sweet. She knew at that moment she'd do anything she could to make his life better.

Now, where in the world did that come from?

Irritated with herself, she got to her feet and hid behind the safety of a giant cherry-veneer desk. "Let me see how things are looking." She used her mouse to look over the latest numbers in their various wings. There were empty rooms in two of them. "We have space available, so I don't see why your father staying here would be a problem."

He sighed. "That's good news. Real good." Before she could say something completely inane, he fastened those eyes on her again. "Susan, would y'all be able to help with his physical therapy?"

"I don't think it would be a problem at all. We help with rehabilitation all the time." She picked up her phone. "Phyllis Morton is in charge of that. I can call her up and see if she can meet with you right now—"

"That's not necessary."

She paused. "Sorry?"

"I, um, don't have time to talk to everyone here today. Just you."

Against her will, her insides turned all mushy. "How about I give you her phone number then? You can talk to her when you have time."

"That would be fine."

"I'll follow up on things, too." She stood and walked around her desk, feeling the need to reassure him.

Or maybe she just wanted to stand a little closer?

He held out his hand. Immediately her hand was surrounded by callused warmth. "Susan, thank you for your time," he murmured. "I'm obliged."

"You're very welcome."

One side of his mouth lifted before he turned away. After a tip of his hat in Paula's direction, he left the building.

And Susan finally exhaled.

When he was out of sight, Paula patted her heart. "Lord have mercy, but that is one fine-looking man."

Wisely, Susan didn't say a word. But privately, well, she was glad she hadn't seen the last of Cal Riddell.

Too anxious and keyed up to get any more work done, she left her office and went on her daily rounds. Several residents were watching *Jeopardy* and good-naturedly calling out answers.

Another group of four were playing cards. Others were reading or doing crosswords. But Rosa Ventura was nowhere to be found. Curious, she walked up to Mrs. Olden, one of Rosa's usual dining partners. "Where's Mrs. Ventura today?"

"We haven't seen her." She shrugged. "I guess she wanted to be alone today."

"Maybe so." Susan kept her expression neutral, but she was growing concerned. Though it wasn't rare for the elderly lady not to be present, it was strange that she hadn't been seen by any of the residents. Usually, the woman made time for everyone and anyone. And was vocal about it, too.

She decided to go to her room and check up on her.

Rosa answered the door after two raps. "What do you want?"

"Nothing. I, uh, was just wondering where you were."

"You found me. I've been here."

Rosa's voice seemed more bitter than usual and her expression looked glum.

"Is anything the matter? Can I come in?"

Still holding the door almost closed, Rosa shook her head sadly. "I appreciate you stopping by, but I'm not in much of a visiting mood today."

Susan didn't know much about the lady except that she liked trivia, cards and had a razor-sharp tongue. "Are you sick?"

For a moment, Rosa looked as though she was going to turn away without answering, but then she sighed. "It's just my anniversary. Some days I miss my husband, that's all."

"I'm sorry. Has he been gone long?"

Rosa nodded. "Four years." With a wave of her hand, she motioned for Susan to move on. "Don't worry, dear. It's just one of those days. I'll be more myself tomorrow."

"I'll count on it," Susan said with a smile.

With a sigh, she walked back to the main room and

played Yahtzee for a few moments, and helped one of the attendants organize the crafts room for a group of Girl Scouts who were stopping by. Finally it was five o'clock.

It had been a busy day.

But, she realized as she walked out to the parking lot, she hardly remembered a thing about it except for Cal Riddell's visit.

"Lord have mercy," she murmured, stealing Paula's line. "What a man."

Chapter Five

"How much longer?"

"We're looking at movies, Hank. Pick one out."

"There's nothing here I want to see. Plus, you've been looking at books, too."

Her son said *books* as if she was looking at Uzis. Though, chances were he'd be way more interested in guns than anything in the library.

"You're just going to have to be patient, Henry," she said as she tried to hold on to her own patience.

Hank turned away with an exaggerated sigh.

Susan felt like doing the same thing. Her boy's feelings about the library were the exact opposite of hers. Sometimes it was hard to come to terms with the fact that he wasn't a reader and had no interest in ever becoming one.

Whenever her mother had taken her to the library, she'd scampered off to the children's section and had gotten lost among the stacks. Without fail, her mother would have to ask her time and again to limit her stack of books to just five. She'd also practically dragged Susan out when it was time to leave.

Hank, however, had stayed by her side from the moment they'd entered. Furthermore, he seemed especially intent on claiming her attention every ten seconds, mainly to encourage her to leave.

"Mom? Mom! Did you see who's here?"

"No. And hush."

Hank pulled on her sleeve. "Mom, it's that man from the hospital."

"Shh," she admonished.

"Mom. Mo-om. Are you listening? He's still there. He's comin' closer."

"I'm listening to you talk too much," she said as sternly as she was able. "We are in the library. You need to be quiet."

"But it's *Mr. Riddell.*"

Just like that, her whole body went tingly. "Oh. Really?"

Funny, how when she was at the Lodge, the only Riddell she thought about was a sixty-two-year-old who could swear up a blue streak.

But when she wasn't working, well, a whole different Riddell man captured her thoughts, and he wore a white Stetson real well.

"Uh-huh. He's standing right over there. Want to go say hey?"

"No, I do not. Besides, we need to leave him alone. A person should be able to go to the library without being pestered."

"Oh, Mom. How are you supposed to make friends if you're always too scared to say hello?"

She was not scared. She was just reserved. And there was nothing wrong with that.... "Hank, let me finish here, and then we'll go get something to eat."

"In a sec. I'll be right back, Mom." In a flash, he left her side and trotted across the aisle to where the new mysteries were shelved. "Hey, Mr. Riddell. Hi! I can't believe I just looked over, and there you were." Without hardly taking a breath, he continued, "I told my mom I saw you, but she said I should leave you alone. But I think she only said that 'cause she didn't want to come over here and say hello."

Susan went from embarrassed to shocked to mortified. Right there in four seconds flat. Way too slowly, her brain caught up with Hank's motormouth and she stilled.

Feeling his icy-hot glare, she turned.

Yes. There he was. Gorgeous in faded jeans, a wrinkled plaid shirt and a pair of scuffed work boots. After reading the inside flap of the book he was holding, Cal leaned down to Hank and almost looked peppy. Well, as peppy as a man who didn't smile could look. "Hey, yourself."

Hank lifted a foot out, almost kicking Cal's shin. "I got me some new boots."

Susan held her breath, waiting for Cal to snap at him.

But instead, he crouched down and looked at the boots carefully. Hank's wide eyes were watching Cal's every movement and facial expression with hope...looking for acceptance.

Oh, her boy so ached for a man's attention!

Cal touched a bit of the embroidery on the leather. "They're very fine. Where'd you get them?"

Hank tucked his chin to his chest. "At the resale shop."

"Ah."

"Mr. Riddell, don't tell nobody. My mom said no one has to know."

"I won't tell a soul," Cal replied, looking as solemn as ever. "You were smart to get them there, I think. Breaking in boots is hard on a man's toes." When he rose to his feet again, Cal looked over her way.

Oh, was she just imagining that his gaze softened?

She edged closer as Hank pulled on his sleeve. "We're runnin' errands today."

"Are you? Like going to the library, huh?"

"Yep. But we gotta go to the grocery store after this."

"You sound real busy."

Worried that Cal was now stuck in a conversation he didn't really want to be in, Susan stepped a little closer. "Well, we'll let you go."

He reached out and touched her arm. "Did you work today?"

"I did."

"How's my dad doing?"

There was true concern in his eyes—and in the undertone of his voice. Cal wasn't just making conversation; he really was worried about his dad.

"He's good." She met his eyes and smiled softly. "Swearing at the physical therapist and flirting with the ladies."

Cal's eyes lit up with relief. "So, nothing new?"

"Nope. Try not to worry," she said, injecting a touch of humor into her voice. "We've got him under control."

"I'll stop by soon. I've been busy." He looked at the book in his hand, and seemed vaguely embarrassed to be caught doing something besides working or looking after his father.

Almost against her will, her heart softened toward him. "Hey. Listen, I'm sorry we bothered you."

"It's no problem." Turning to Hank, his voice turned a shade warmer. "Glad you showed me your boots."

That voice. So gravelly. So masculine. It got under her skin and curled her toes. "I wouldn't have thought you'd frequent the library."

His eyes narrowed. "Why?"

She stumbled for a reply. Now she felt stupid. "No reason." When he still looked her over in confusion, Susan felt like the rudest woman ever. "I mean, I guess I would have thought you'd be the type of man to just go buy a book."

He stared at her with those cool blue-gray eyes, which made her dig the hole she was in that much deeper. "I mean... Shoot. I mean, oh, never mind. I was trying to be cute, but it sounded like an insult—I don't know why."

"Electra doesn't have a bookstore, beyond Walmart and such. Did you know that?"

"I did."

"And I like to read."

"I do, too." As his gaze strayed to the four DVDs clutched in her hands, Susan felt her cheeks color. "Hank, not so much."

Hank was staring up at Cal as if something earth-shattering was going to pop out of the cowboy's mouth any moment.

Cal glanced down at him and said, "Serena, Jarred's girlfriend, is the librarian here. Did you know that?" Hank shook his head. "She's great. You ought to get to know her."

Instead of nodding politely, Hank just kicked at the carpet with the point of his boot. "Reading's boring. It sucks."

Cal narrowed his eyes.

Half an aisle down, a woman gasped. Whether it was from Hank's continual chatter, or his words...Susan didn't know.

She felt her cheeks heat. "I think that's my cue to move on."

To her embarrassment, Cal's silence seemed to make Hank think it was fine to keep on talking. "This place sucks, too," he said a little bit louder, all full of masculine bravado.

"Gentlemen watch their mouths around ladies, son."

A sheen of red tinted Hank's cheeks, but he didn't back down. "I'm not a gentleman. I'm just a kid."

Susan laughed it off. "We'll just get out of your way."

"You weren't in my way at all," Cal corrected softly. And with that, he tipped his hat at Susan, turned and walked to a shelf of mysteries, obviously in no hurry to speak to her anymore.

Susan usually would have said something—anything— to defend herself and her son. But in truth, she wondered where Hank's sudden burst of mouthiness came from.

Trying to remember when it had started, she thought it might have been when his diabetes had been diagnosed. Had she begun to let him get away with more and more when she'd felt so bad for him?

"Come on, Hank. Let's go check these movies out."

In an uncharacteristic move, Hank nodded silently and walked to the circulation desk. His lips were in full pout by the time she swiped their card and they strode out to her SUV.

When they were buckled in, he looked her way. "Do you think Mr. Riddell likes me?" he asked quietly.

Her first impulse was to say of course he did. But then maybe he didn't. "I think he does," she replied finally, after she backed out of her parking space. "He's just not a real demonstrative guy."

"He liked my boots. Don't you think?"

"I know he did."

"Do you really think his father told him that stuff?"

"What stuff?"

"That stuff about ladies and gentlemen…"

"I imagine so. It's the kind of thing some dads teach their sons. Especially here in Texas, I suppose."

"Why?"

"Why? Because people go through life trying not to hurt other people's feelings, that's why." She shook her head. "You shouldn't have told him that the library and reading sucks. Mr. Riddell obviously likes to read. There's a saying that goes, if you don't have anything nice to say, then you shouldn't say anything at all." There, now she could teach manners, too.

Of course, she doubted her lessons were going to have the impact she'd been hoping for.

Hank was silent until they reached the grocery store. As they walked to the front door, he turned her way again. "Do you think you'll see him again soon?"

"I suppose so. I work where his dad is getting physical therapy. Don't worry about him anymore, honey."

By her side, Hank didn't respond, though she noticed a tightening to his jaw. He was stewing.

Oh, but she wished it was already ten o'clock. Then she'd be getting ready to take a bath and put this day behind her. It had been a difficult one—Kay had been especially short-tempered and on her case. Rosa Ventura had been moody and had hurt two other ladies' feelings.

And Mr. Calvin Riddell was proving to make his son Cal seem like an angel. He was demanding and short-tempered and mean.

And because of all those things, she was having to step in all the time and smooth things over. And he'd only been there one day.

"When we get home, let's make mac and cheese," Hank said.

All those carbs would wreak havoc with his blood sugar levels, but there was a chance they could make it work. "We'll do a test, and if things look good, then we'll get out that blue box."

"'Kay," he murmured, finally turning agreeable.

Susan tried to think of that as a positive thing—or

maybe it really wasn't. Maybe it was just that he was at the end of his rope, too. Tired and more than ready to take a break from life.

Chapter Six

Later that night, hours after fingers had been stuck, glucose meter read, insulin shot given, Hank's favorite TV shows had been watched, and he was in bed, Susan's neighbor came knocking on the door.

"Am I interrupting anything?" Betsy asked as soon as Susan greeted her at the door.

"Just an old rerun of *Law & Order*."

Looking over her shoulder, Betsy grimaced at the television. "Oh, my word."

Susan glanced at the screen. On TV were two detectives leaning over a particularly gruesome-looking dead body. "What?"

"If that doesn't turn your stomach, nothing will," Betsy said as she walked on in and closed the door behind her. "Susan, you are completely incorrigible, girl. Turn that off."

Dutifully, she did just that, then turned to her friend. "Is there a reason you came over? Or were you just needing someone to boss around for a while?"

"I needed some advice, actually. Do you mind listening to me for a little bit?"

Betsy looked younger than usual, with her outfit of black yoga pants, loose violet-gray tank top and worried expression. Most of her makeup had been washed off, and her usually spiky hair was brushed back.

Getting to her feet, Susan walked to the kitchen. "I've got a bottle of wine. I'll open it."

After pouring two glasses, they bypassed the living room and sat together on the padded window seat in the breakfast nook. It was the farthest sitting area from the bedrooms. Though it wasn't likely that they'd wake Hank up, Susan didn't want to chance it. Hank needed his sleep.

And she, well, she needed girl time like nobody's business. "So, what's up?"

Betsy leaned her head back against the window as if she had the weight of the world on her shoulders. After a sigh and a sip, however, a new resolution lit her eyes. "So, do you remember that night I went out clubbing while you stayed home?"

"I do. That's the night you went to the honky-tonk, right? The one where Cal Riddell was supposed to be at?"

"That's the very one."

"And, did everything go okay?" Susan started thinking all about worst-case scenarios. Had Betsy danced with Cal and fallen in love?

"It went better than that. Susan, I think I fell in love."

"With whom?" Even as she asked the question, her stomach knotted. Even though chances were slim that Betsy had even met Cal, Susan found herself bracing for the worst possible news.

"Gene Howard. Do you know him?"

"No." She exhaled, feeling almost giddy. When Betsy's eyebrows rose, Susan said, "I mean, no, I've never heard of him. You know I don't know too many people under eighty."

"He's dreamy."

Betsy's comment teased a smile. "Dreamy, huh? Now,

that's a description I haven't heard in a while. How dreamy is he?"

Betsy fanned herself dramatically. "Dreamy enough to make me think of diamond rings and honeymoons."

"After a meeting in a bar? Don't you think that's kind of sudden?"

"Of course. I know it's crazy, but he's just so great. Plus, he's from Amarillo."

"From Amarillo, huh? What does he do?"

"Something to do with selling to supermarket chains. It's a good job. Marrying a guy like that would be perfect. I'd be set for life."

Marrying a guy for his money seemed awfully cold, though Susan couldn't deny that a tiny part of her understood Betsy's motives. Bills and hunger did have a way of coming to the surface in every relationship. "Do you have plans to see him soon?"

"Actually, I do," Betsy replied with a grin.

Susan sipped her wine and studied her friend some more. Maybe it was because she was so out of practice dating, but she couldn't fathom what had spurred the visit. "What's wrong?"

Setting her glass of wine down, Betsy looked directly at Susan. "See, the thing of it is...ol' Gene thinks I'm a lot more like you than, well...me."

"What are you talking about?"

"See, the thing of it is...Gene doesn't know I've been around the block a time or two." She bit her lip. "Or twenty. As soon as I started getting the idea that he's on the conservative side, I started telling him all about how I rarely go out to bars. How I usually stay home at night and watch old television shows." She frowned. "Things kind of spun out of control after that."

"There's nothing wrong with you, Betsy. I stay home

because I have Hank and because I like to watch TV on the couch. It's nothing to try to emulate."

"I know that. But for some reason, there at the bar, I just started spouting half truths like nobody's business. Gene seems to really like the idea of me being able to cook." Looking despondent, she added, "Gene can't wait to taste my pecan pie."

"Pecan pie? Do you even bake?"

"Not yet. I'm going to have to practice baking all the time now."

"Not if you tell him the truth."

After pretty much gulping the rest of her wine, Betsy said, "I would. But, Susan, I'm so tired of being alone, you know?"

Unfortunately, she knew about that feeling all too well. "What are you going to do now?"

Betsy's eyes lit up. "I have a plan. Gene likes to double-date. Him and me and you and Steve."

Full-fledged panic set in. "Who the heck is Steve?"

"His widowed neighbor."

This was getting worse and worse. "Oh, Betsy."

"Come on, it won't be so bad."

"It won't be so good." Susan imagined sitting at a restaurant with Betsy and two men, all the while Betsy pretending she was Betty Crocker and Susan pretending she still remembered how to talk about anything other than work.

"Susan, please say you will. If you go out with us, I can kind of follow your lead. When you talk about working with old people all day, I can act like that's interesting."

This time it was Susan who was chugging her wine. Was that really how Betsy saw her? As a boring woman who watched reruns on TV, never went out and only hung out with people old enough to be her parents…or grand-parents?

"Listen, Betsy, if Gene asked you out again, he obviously likes you. And it's probably for a whole lot more reasons than him wanting a piece of pecan pie. Just be yourself. He'll be glad to know you."

Betsy looked appalled. "Hell, no, he won't. He thinks I'm sweet, like you." Mumbling under her breath, she added, "He thinks I'm almost virginal."

"Um, I have Hank, Betsy. I really did give birth to him. I'm no virgin."

"You're close, though." She scratched her head. "Ever since you've moved in, you work and take care of Hank. That's it. What's more, you don't even act like you're sad about missing out on dating."

"Hey, now—"

But Betsy just kept talking. "You don't even act like you're sad about not getting all hot and bothered between the sheets."

"I don't…all that much," she admitted.

"Why not? Do you not like sex?"

Oh, this was horrible. "I like it fine." Well, she did… back when she *was* having sex. Seven years ago.

"But you don't miss it?"

Of course she did! But, well, she missed a lot of things. She missed feeling pretty and having someone to get pretty for. She missed candlelight and sweet, suggestive smiles. She missed anticipation.

But all she ever got by "missing" was yet another bout of sadness and melancholy. "I can't afford to miss things," she murmured. "I have a son."

"But there's got to be more to it than that."

Was there? Suddenly, all the reasons she'd shut down on

life didn't seem to make that much sense. Was she afraid of getting hurt again? Afraid to dream again?

Perhaps she was so twisted that she was even afraid to *want* to dream again. And that answer, of course, made her reply sharper than she meant to. "Not really. I don't have the money or the time to get dolled up and think about dating. More important, I don't have the emotional strength for it, either."

Remembering how betrayed she'd felt by Greg, she muttered, "Sometimes I think there's just nothing left inside me for romance."

Slowly Betsy put down her wineglass. "I'm sorry. You always sound so positive about your life. I guess I never really took the time to think that you don't really feel that way."

"Don't make me into someone I'm not. I'm fine. And one day, I'm sure I'll meet somebody and everything will be all good. But right now, it's all on hold."

"That could be years, Susan."

"It doesn't matter." Thinking about Greg, and the big mistake she'd made with him, Susan added, "It's not like I haven't lived. Obviously I've been around the block a time or two myself."

"I have a feeling those blocks you've been around aren't all that big."

"Maybe you're right." For the first time in a long while, Susan gave herself permission to stop feeling so guilty about the choices she'd been making in life. "Maybe they weren't all that big at all."

"So…do you think there's any chance I can get you to change your mind about this double date?"

"Nope."

Betsy winked. "It might be good practice for Mr. Right."

"I'm not up for practicing," she said with a smile, though it felt strained.

Because all of a sudden, Cal Riddell flashed in her mind. He was the type of man women dreamed about. Correction. He was the man *she'd* been dreaming about. Steady, responsible.

Handsome.

Oh, they had their differences. And maybe that's all they would ever have. But his very being had made her think of…getting all hot and bothered between the sheets. And though she wasn't looking for an easy love like Betsy, Susan realized that sometime during the last few weeks she'd started thinking about living again.

Ever since she'd had Hank, she'd put everything about herself in a drawer. Keeping it shut away while she tried her best to do what was right for the two of them.

With force, she'd done her best to ignore feelings of desire. She'd looked away and coolly ignored flirtations with the few men she'd met. That wasn't who she was.

Actually, that wasn't who she was *now*.

But maybe one day she'd meet a man like Cal who would like her back. Then, she could become the woman she'd always dreamed of being but had never imagined was possible.

Chapter Seven

With a grunt, Cal lifted another bag of feed onto his shoulder and carried it to the empty stall at the end of the barn. Each bag was fifty pounds, and there were a dozen of them. After carrying four, he'd broken a sweat.

By the seventh, Cal had a pounding headache.

As he walked the feed to the stall and then laid it down neatly on the others, he turned around and stretched, wincing slightly as his head continued to pound.

Too much coffee and not enough sleep did that to a person, he supposed. That and the constant worrying about things he couldn't control.

With another grunt, he bent down and hefted another sack onto his shoulder. Dust and particles of straw blew up into his face. Balancing the bag on one shoulder, he wiped his eyes with his bandanna, then started walking. When he passed Jet, the old palomino whinnied softly.

"I know," he told the horse. "I'm getting a little old for this, aren't I?"

Usually, he would've asked one of the hands to take care of the new feed they were adding to the horses' diet. But he'd needed something to take the edge off this morning. Unfortunately, the physical labor didn't seem to be doing the trick.

Back and forth he went, another two times. Thinking all the while about his conversation with Trent.

Last night, he'd spoken to his brother for almost half an hour, and it had been completely frustrating. Every time he'd asked Trent specifics about his injuries, his brother laughed him off.

Yet again.

So all Cal knew was that his little brother was going into surgery this morning. The doctors were worried that his fever had spiked, and some of his other tests weren't positive.

Trent—being Trent—had acted as if it was no big deal, but there was an edge to his voice that worried Cal. "How about I come out and visit with you for a bit? I can be on a plane in three hours."

But his brother had only laughed. "What are you going to do when you get here? Watch me sleep?"

"Maybe. You probably need somebody there to check up on your progress, don't you think? To make sure you're doing what you're supposed to do." But even to his ears, his words sounded awkward and stilted. His brother had been doing just fine on the rodeo circuit without an older brother's meddling.

"Junior, I don't need a keeper."

"I know...."

"Uh-huh."

"I'm just trying to help, that's all."

"Oh, is that what it's called? You're acting like the only person who knows how to do things right is you. But that wasn't the case back when I was walking in your shadow on the ranch, and it sure as hell ain't the case now."

Satisfied that his chore was done, Cal strode into the washroom, rinsed his face and hands, then finally retreated to his office in the barn.

And thought some more about that phone call.

After Trent had delivered that little zinger, he'd gripped the phone harder.

Why did Trent always bring up the past when he got pissed off? "I didn't say I was right and you were wrong." Truly, all he was doing was trying to make his brother's life easier.

"You didn't need to. I heard it in your voice, plain as day. I tell you, I'm fine. Listen to me, will you?"

"I'm listening." Oh, but he was so tired of fighting with everyone. With his dad. With Ginny. With Susan Young. Because he could practically smell the smoke coming out of Trent's ears, he'd swallowed his pride a bit more. "I'm sorry if I offended."

Now that he'd gotten his way, Trent's voice had turned smooth. "No, it's okay. I know you mean well. And having a keeper probably wouldn't be that bad of an idea, actually. But if I do need one, I can find my own."

"How so?"

Trent's voice had lifted. "Shoot, you know how. I'll get on the phone and call for help. There's plenty of ladies around here who'd love to hold my hand and whisper sweet things in my ear."

Oh, that was what Trent needed, all right. "Wait a minute—"

"I'm not eight and I'm not eighty-eight, Cal. Don't make me into you."

"Me?"

"Ever since Christy went and broke your heart, you've been living like a monk."

Christy hadn't broken his heart. She'd just showed him that women changed their minds. Only taught him that *forever* didn't necessarily mean *forever with him*.

No, sometimes it only meant *forever, until something better came along*.

But he didn't need his little brother bringing it up. "Hey, now—"

But Trent had just kept talking. "Now, living all clean and sober might be fine for you, but it's not for me. I'll be fine. I can talk to doctors without your help, and I can get a nice lady to help me with anything else I need, too. We both know you've got Dad to worry about, and that's enough for anyone."

"I hear you. But you will call me if you need it?"

"Always. I always do."

There was a surety in his brother's voice that had calmed Cal, and made him not eager to push things. Though Trent was as different from Cal as night from day, there was still that pecking order from childhood that couldn't be ignored.

Jarred was the most like their parents. Fun loving, easygoing.

Trent was the most like the family's dreams—larger than life, shiny and new.

And Cal? Well, for some reason he was like his grandfather. The man who made do with little. He'd been responsible. A worrier. Nowadays, it was Cal Jr. who balanced the checkbook, worked on investments and made sure the millions of dollars the Riddells now had wouldn't ever go away.

It was a lot of responsibility, and he took it seriously.

Someone had to do it.

But every once in a while, Cal couldn't help but envy his little brother. Envy Trent's celebrity status and his movie-star looks and his ease with the ladies.

And his ease with life. Trent Riddell didn't worry about a thing he didn't have to. Ever.

Cal wished he'd inherited even a smidge of that gumption. Somehow, he'd inherited too much responsibility. Too much caution. Duty seemed to be what he was all about. Duty and promises.

Which was why he couldn't sleep at night. It was why he carried feed bags at five in the morning and checked on all their financial holdings by six-thirty.

AND IT WAS ALSO WHY HE was walking into the Electra Lodge bright and early at 8:00 a.m. with a head that was threatening to self-destruct in seconds, not minutes. Even though he was wishing he was somewhere else, someone had to sit in the rehab center and deal with their cantankerous father.

Even if that someone always seemed to be him.

Mrs. Lawson, the administrator, greeted him at the door. "Good morning, Mr. Riddell."

From the moment they met, Cal had respected the woman. She was competent and polite and seemed to care for all the residents.

But though she was striking, and not much older than Susan, he knew he wasn't attracted to her in the slightest. "Please just call me Cal. Or Junior. Mr. Riddell is my dad."

"I'll be happy to do that." Her eyes sparkled. "Especially since I don't think I could ever confuse the two of you. I mean this in the best way when I say that you're nothing like your father."

"Uh-oh. Has he been behaving himself?"

"He's nothing we can't handle," Mrs. Lawson said evasively.

Looking over to the receptionist, she said, "Paula, would you mind walking Cal down to see his father?"

"Sure thing, Kay." After standing up and walking around her desk, Paula gave him a friendly smile. "How you doing, Junior?"

"I'm good."

"How's Trent doing?" Paula, all permed hair and blushing cheeks, had been hanging on to Trent's arm at Bob's last summer like a hooked catfish. No matter how hard Trent had tried to shake her, she hadn't seemed willing to be let go.

Though, maybe, Trent hadn't tried all that hard.

Anyway, Cal had been sure he was going to wake up and find Paula in their kitchen. Luckily, he hadn't. He never knew if Trent had gotten together with Paula, and he liked it that way.

"He's all right."

"That's not what I heard. I heard from Betsy he was injured."

"He was. A bull got the best of him in New Mexico."

Her eyes widened. "Is he going to be okay?"

"Yes. Well, he will when he gets out of surgery."

"Maybe I should call him. You know, to see if he needs anything."

"I don't think so, Paula. He's really not up for phone calls."

Paula stopped, obviously waiting for more information, but he was in no mood to give her anything. His worries about his brother were personal, and he was in no hurry to discuss Trent with Paula in the middle of the hall. Clearing his throat, he said, "I stopped by to visit my dad. Ms. Lawson said he's settling in okay?"

"More or less." With a slow smile, she said, "Some days are better than others."

"That sounds about right."

"Some things with your daddy never change. I remember before y'all struck oil. Your father was as scrappy as they came."

"He still is." He paused, wondering what else he could

say. He wasn't real fond of talking about his father's faults with Paula.

"Cal?"

He turned so fast, he almost got whiplash. "Susan."

Paula stilled. "Hey, Susan. I was just going to take Junior here to see his father."

"Ah." Humor lit her eyes.

Cal narrowed his. Wordlessly, he sent out a plaintive SOS.

A second passed. Then Susan turned all calm, cool and professional. "Cal, would you mind if I walked the rest of the way with you? I had something I wanted to discuss."

"I wouldn't mind at all." Stepping to her side, he breathed a sigh of relief. After saying goodbye to Paula, they walked in silence until they turned the corner.

Then, when it was obvious no one else was around, he stopped for a moment and leaned against the cool tiles that covered the wall. "She was driving me crazy."

"I could tell." To his pleasure, Susan took a place next to him on the wall. The muscles in her neck visibly relaxed when she smiled his way. "You were looking like a cornered dog by her side."

"She—like half the female population—has a crush on my brother. I get tired of fielding Trent questions."

To his surprise, and pleasure, she giggled.

He almost smiled. "Is my pain amusing you, Ms. Young?"

"Definitely." Turning her head so their eyes met, she smiled again. "I'm going to have to do this more often."

"Do what?"

"Just lean against the wall and laugh. Relax for a second."

"You should." Letting his gaze settle on her, he drawled,

"I'm beginning to get the impression that you work too hard."

"Oh, no harder than most everyone else. But leaning against the wall, out of everyone's sight, kind of feels good." She shimmied a bit against the cool tiles for emphasis.

He made the mistake of watching those hips.

And *pow!* Just like that, his breath caught. She was really a pretty thing. And the way she was leaning up there against the wall, well, it brought to mind a whole wealth of ideas. None of which was appropriate.

But still, he couldn't stop looking. And wondering. Until Susan, he'd never had a thing for redheads. Now he was starting to think he'd completely underestimated the allure of long auburn hair. And those green eyes of hers never failed to show every single emotion she was feeling.

She glanced at him and caught him staring. "What?"

"Nothing. I was just thinking that I'm glad our paths crossed again."

She smiled as she stepped away from the wall and straightened her skirt. "I am, too. The more we talk to each other, the more I'm glad we've met. Especially when we're not snapping at each other."

He winced. "That's been my fault. I've been in a snappy mood. Everything with my dad—it's gotten under my skin. I hope I wasn't too hard on your son. I get used to correcting Ginny."

Something in her eyes flickered. "He was fine. Hank's heard worse." She stepped closer as they started walking again. "Ginny is just six, right?"

"Uh-huh." He couldn't help but roll his eyes. "She's six going on sixteen."

To his pleasure, Susan chuckled at that. "She's a handful?"

"That's putting it mildly."

Her eyes softened. Almost hesitantly, she touched his elbow. "Don't worry. All little girls ache to be six going on sixteen at one time or another. Before you know it she'll be her regular self."

"That's what I'm afraid of!"

She shared a smile with him as they continued toward his father's room. A little farther down, they passed two open doorways. One was a bedroom; a nurse or someone looked to be visiting. Another was a storage closet.

Two elderly women were inside, staring at the top shelf. When Susan and Cal approached, one of the women tagged Susan. "Just who we needed to see."

"Yes?"

"Can you help us get this Monopoly game down?"

Before she could comply, Cal stepped in and easily pulled the board game off the top shelf. "Here you are, ladies. Where may I take it for you?"

"Junior! Look at you." The women looked at him, and then at Susan. "You can just hand it to me," the shorter of the two said. "We aren't so far gone that we can't carry games."

"You two going to play Monopoly today, Mrs. Carriage?"

"Not by ourselves, dear. A few seventh graders are stopping by." With a wink to Cal, she added, "They come here thinking they're doing good with community service. We take turns beating them at board games."

"I'm impressed," Cal said.

"We try," Mrs. Carriage said lightly. "Have to show those kids we haven't lost our minds." Stepping closer, she gave Cal a friendly perusal. "So…Junior…are you and Susan keeping company now?"

As he was figuring how to answer that one, Susan

jumped in. "Oh, no. Cal's just here to see his father. His father's here for a bit. I'm sorry. Did y'all know each other?"

Mrs. Carriage looked him over as if he were prime real estate. "I've known Calvin for quite a while. And of course I know you by sight, Junior. But I don't believe the two of us have ever conversed." One eyebrow arched. "Or have I forgotten that pleasure?"

"No, ma'am."

"How's Trent doing? Still riding bulls?"

Sometimes it took him by surprise, the way everyone knew his family's business. "He is. Doing real well, too. Well, until this past week. A cussed bull named Diablo got the best of him."

He felt Susan's gaze settle on him. But didn't have a chance to explain because Mrs. Cousins had sidled up in between them. "Oh, dear. I hope he's okay."

"He's mending. I'll let him know you asked after him."

"Aren't you a sweetheart? You know, you sure are a lot more polite than your daddy."

"I've been told that a time or two."

Turning to Susan, who'd been watching the interplay with a curious expression on her face, he said, "Ready?"

"Oh. Of course. Your dad's just down here." Ten steps later, they were outside his father's room. In the silence of the hall, he was even more aware of her.

She seemed just as affected. Her eyes rested briefly on his lips. Then she swallowed. "Uh, Cal, please let me know if you need anything. Anything at all."

Though the words were suggestive, he fought to not read anything into what she was saying. "Thank you. I will."

"Okay, then. I better let you go so you can have your visit."

He held out his hand, intending to give her a friendly

handshake. "I appreciate you walking me down here." Her hand was slim and cool.

She looked him over almost shyly but kept her hand in his. Almost as if she didn't want to leave his side. Then she looked away again. "Okay. Well, uh, if I don't see you later, have a good evening."

"You, too." Before he thought better of it, he tugged at her slightly, bringing her a little closer. Close enough to brush his lips against her cheek.

In a sweet way. Almost platonic.

Except he couldn't remember the last time he'd brushed his lips against any woman's cheek.

"Oh!" she said.

He let go of her hand. "Thanks again."

"You're welcome." She turned away. He had only a moment to admire the way her slacks curved around her bottom in just the right way, when she faced him again. "You know what? You can actually be nice."

"That's true. Matter of fact, I've even heard some say that I'm nicer than most," he added to tease her a bit. She grinned at that, then, obviously tongue-tied, spun and walked away. Suddenly he wished he'd thought to give her a compliment right back.

Because there was a whole lot he could have complimented her on. Her gorgeous hair falling in thick waves halfway down her back. Her figure, which was something out of a 1950s pinup calendar.

Or maybe it was her demeanor here at the Lodge. The way she put up with the many people who seemed to want a piece of her, who needed answers immediately. The way she knew pretty much everyone by name, whether it was the maintenance staff or one of the directors.

The way she didn't complain, and the way she always had a kind word for everyone.

How come he was just noticing these things? Had she been hiding these qualities from him? Or had he been the one who was so stressed that he had only looked for her worst traits?

Right then and there Cal knew Susan Young was someone he wanted to get to know a whole lot better.

A little shocked at the thought, Cal paused before knocking on his father's door. "Dad, how you doing?"

His father was sitting in a wheelchair, looking pissed off at the world. "Worse than you, by the looks of things. You seem almost happy, Junior."

Cal tried to scowl, but he couldn't. "Is that a problem?"

"Not at all. Just for a while now, I've been starting to think you had given up smiling for good."

"Thanks for letting me know."

"So what's the reason?"

How could he explain everything he was thinking about Susan—when he wasn't even sure what his feelings really were?

And besides, Cal had come to check up on his dad. To help ease his burdens. "We don't need to talk about me."

"Sure we do. I'm sick and tired of everyone worried about my body. Come here, boy, and take a seat."

It was enough of a command that Cal obeyed.

But there was also enough love and care in his voice for Cal to do what his dad asked. Perching on the end of his father's bed, he started talking. "There's this woman... She's becoming a friend." Did a handful of conversations count as friendship? He shook his head in confusion. "Maybe she's almost a friend."

His father rolled his eyes. "Sounds serious."

Cal supposed he deserved that one. "I know I'm not making any sense. It's just that she caught me off guard."

"And you hate that."

He did. "I didn't see it coming."

"So who is this woman?"

There was no reason to lie. "Susan Young. She works here. Do you know her? She's got red hair."

To his surprise, his dad's expression softened. "I don't know her name, but I'd recognize her anywhere. That girl's a sight for sore eyes, I'll tell you that. Trent would say she's a hottie."

Hottie? Never again did he want to hear that word come out of his dad's mouth.

And he didn't appreciate his father even commenting on Susan's looks, either. "You know, there's a whole lot more to her than looks."

"I imagine so," his father said drily.

Cal tried again. "Susan's a nice lady. I met her when I was visiting you at the hospital. She's got a son who was just diagnosed with diabetes. I'm afraid we got off on the wrong foot."

"Ain't hard to do in the hospital," his father said softly. "Being in those sanitized, bare rooms puts me in a bad mood just about the minute I get there. I have a feeling you might be the same way."

"Maybe that was it. I don't know."

"But now?"

"Now we just had a halfway-decent conversation. It was nice." It had also brought forth a whole host of feelings he hadn't realized he was still capable of feeling.

Tenderness toward her. Protective instincts. And, well, good old-fashioned lust. He ached to kiss her.

But he wasn't sharing any of that with his dad.

Standing up, he shook his head. "Dad, I know you don't need me to be going on and on about a woman. How about we take a turn around this place?"

"I'd rather hear about the woman." He paused. "Truth

is, I'd just about decided that you were going to live out your life as some kind of lone wolf."

"Lone wolf, huh?"

"You have to admit, it's been a while since you've mentioned any woman. Any woman besides Christy."

"Christy was trouble."

"She was. With a capital *T.* I know she hurt you when she dumped you for another man—but you can't give up on life, Junior. I mean, take your brother."

Still trying to keep his expression impassive after his father's extremely succinct review of his love life, Cal said, "Jarred or Trent?"

"Jarred, of course. Now, he and Serena are real happy together. Nothing wrong with that, you know. Maybe you should think about finding a gal."

"I don't have time."

"But this Susan…"

"She's just a friend. That's all. Come on, Dad. Let's get out of this room. I want some coffee."

"I'll agree to that, as long as you help me find Rosa Ventura. I intend to razz her every chance I get."

Now, there was a story. "My pleasure."

Chapter Eight

Cal Riddell Jr. was way too attractive for his own good. Nearly everyone at the Lodge seemed to be charmed by him.

To make things even more perplexing, Susan was fairly sure the cowboy was completely unaware of the power of his charisma.

As they'd walked around the halls and spoken with both residents and staff, he'd been nothing but polite. Not the least bit flirty—not even with Paula.

However, he'd acted far differently toward her.

Yes, with her, he'd given his full complete attention. She'd seen it in the way he had patiently waited for her to speak. With how he'd kept pace with her stride, never rushing her. He'd held doors open for her and had stood politely when one or more people had needed her attention. As though he'd had nothing else to do but see to her needs.

And she'd felt his gaze, heating up just a little bit too much when she'd playfully leaned against the wall. Her cheek still felt tingly from where his lips had brushed it.

For a while there, she'd felt beautiful.

Oh, her mirror had always let her know she wasn't ugly. Susan knew she had pretty hair. And she'd always been partial to her green eyes, as well.

But sometime over the past few years, she'd become more and more insecure about herself. Worse, she'd started to doubt her worth in the relationship department. And Hank's dad had made damn sure she had lost most of her trust in relationships. Since then, she'd always been so unsure about her looks, and about men's motives around her. Over time, she'd immediately assumed that the problem had been at least partly her fault.

But some of those insecurities had slowly begun to fade when she was around Cal. His complete masculinity made her feel feminine. His innate confidence bolstered her pride.

To her surprise, Susan found herself smiling back at him when they were walking together down the hall. The barbs they'd traded had made her laugh, not hurt.

And even though he made her nervous—because she was suddenly feeling things she hadn't thought she could feel anymore—Susan felt more at ease with him than she could ever remember feeling with any man.

Which was really pretty scary. It wasn't as if they had anything going on between them. At all. They were simply cautious acquaintances.

Well, maybe a little more than that.

As SHE SAT BACK BEHIND her computer screen, Susan felt antsy. She was sick of entering information on the database. What she really wanted to do was check to see how Cal was doing with his dad.

She bit her lip and stared as the rows of columns blurred, making her head pound but her spirits lift.

Her body was telling her that she *needed* to get out of this chair.

She almost smiled.

"Susan, I'm leaving for the day."

Startled, she looked up to spy her boss standing in the doorway with her purse in one hand and a glow in her eyes. "All right," she said. Tilting her head to one side, Susan examined Kay more closely. "Hey, you look happy."

"I am. My husband and I are going to the movies and dinner tonight."

"Well, I hope you have a good time."

"I'm sure we will." But Kay only made it two steps out the door before backtracking. "Oh, please don't forget to check in with the kitchen staff when you make your rounds." She bit her lip. "And there were some nursing issues that were supposed to be resolved. You might need to check with them."

"I will."

A wrinkle formed between her brows. "And Joan in the gift shop looked like she might need a visit today. She's a volunteer, you know, but I don't think anyone's thanked her for a while."

Standing up, Susan gave her boss a little wave. "I'll do that. Now, I'll see you tomorrow."

Susan practically held her breath as she and the receptionist watched Kay exit the building, race out toward the parking lot, get in her car and finally leave. Only then did she exhale.

"I didn't think she was ever going to actually leave," Paula said with a relieved smile.

"I'm glad she did. I think she worked sixty hours last week."

Still looking out the window, Paula asked, "Where did Kay go off to in such a hurry? Did she tell you?"

"She did," Susan said with a smile. "She's going out on a date with her husband."

"That's sweet." Though her phone was blinking, Paula leaned back in her chair and continued to look out the window. "She's only recently remarried. Did you know that?"

Susan was floored. "Not at all."

"Yep. She married Scott just eight months ago." Paula frowned. "Oh, her first husband was such a jerk! He had an affair. We were all heartbroken for her."

Completely sucked in to the story, Susan leaned against the receptionist's desk and settled in. "So she tossed him out?"

"Uh-huh. But she was just devastated, I'll tell you that. For a while there, we didn't know if she was ever going to recover. She worked here nonstop, hardly even smiling the whole time."

"I bet that was difficult for you." Susan knew how hard it was to work with someone who was in a permanent bad mood.

"It was. Kay wasn't terrible to work for, she just wasn't happy, you know? There was a gloom settling over this place that even Mr. Price, the owner, was worried about."

"But then she met her husband?"

Paula grinned with all the confidence of someone in the know. "He came in with his aunt and he and Kay immediately hit it off. It was something to see. Within days of their first date, she was glowing."

"And now they go on dinner dates." Susan did her best to act as if she wasn't in the slightest jealous of her boss's romantic story.

Paula looked her up and down. "Speaking of all that, Cal Riddell is still here."

"Oh?" Susan had no idea why Paula thought she would care.

"Oh, yes." With a grin, the blue-eyed blonde made a shooing motion with her hands. "Since you're finally off your computer, you might as well make sure you stop by to see how he's doing."

Susan wanted to see him…but she didn't want to be a pest, either. "I think I'll wait a bit. After all, he's here to see his father."

"But he's in the game room with him. One of the residents just told me that boy is pure magic with his dad."

"How so?"

"He's somehow managing to make that father of his almost pleasant to be around. Halfway social."

"That's quite an accomplishment. Well, then. I guess I had better go take a walk around. Just to see how he's doing."

Susan tried to pretend that she was calm, cool and collected, but she knew she was fooling no one. Not even herself.

After a cursory tour through the kitchens, where she found out that they would, indeed, need to hire three more servers, and a visit to the nursing director, she stopped by to see Joan at the gift shop.

For the next few minutes, Joan told Susan all about her two sons and their busy families. Susan was genuinely interested and even chuckled at a story Joan told about her oldest son's set of twins.

She found Cal sitting at a table nursing a cup of coffee while his father played gin with Rosa Ventura.

So far, very few of her conversations with the older Riddell had been enjoyable. Calvin Riddell Sr. was smart as a whip, and had a tongue just about as sharp, and that was a fact.

Cal Sr. looked up when she approached, and grunted.

His son, on the other hand, smiled. "Hey. I was wondering if you were going to stop by."

"I probably should be in a chair behind my computer, but I get tired of sitting in that room."

"I know I would." Oh, darn! There was that slight zing between them that set her toes on fire.

Feeling as if both Rosa and Mr. Riddell were watching them with interest, Susan turned away. "Hi, Mrs. Ventura. Hello, Mr. Riddell. How are you two doing today?"

"Well enough," Rosa said.

Mr. Riddell skipped the pleasantries. "Well enough to be stuck playing with someone who cheats."

Rosa narrowed her eyes. "Pardon me?"

"You heard," Cal Sr. barked as he discarded. "Don't try and pretend you didn't."

Susan sucked in a breath as Rosa looked ready to explode.

"I do not cheat," she said huffily as she rearranged the cards in her hand.

"You must. There's no other way to explain why you've been beating me."

"There's the obvious," she blurted as she drew another card. "You're not very good at gin."

Cal Jr. pulled forward a chair and motioned for Susan to take a seat. "They've been this way for almost an hour," he murmured. "It would be entertaining if I wasn't afraid they were going to kill each other."

"Yikes," she whispered. Just as Rosa called out "gin" and Mr. Riddell slammed his cards on the table and let out a few choice curse words.

Susan found herself blushing, though Rosa simply raised her eyebrows. "I never knew that maneuver was possible, Cal. Maybe you should demonstrate it."

"Maybe I should," Mr. Riddell retorted. "It would serve you right."

"Oh, boy," Susan murmured.

After looking at her, Cal cleared his throat. "Dad, you can't talk like that around here. There're ladies present. Behave yourself."

"I'm behaving."

Rosa sniffed. Cal scowled.

"I'm behaving well enough," Mr. Riddell amended. He drummed his fingers on the table as a new gleam entered his eyes. "So when I haven't been losing at cards, I've been trying to get some information out of my son about you."

Across from him, Rosa calmly picked up the cards and shuffled. "He's been relentless," she added.

"Not so much. Just curious."

"What have you found out?"

"Well, for starters, Junior here told me you have a son."

"I do." As always happened when she thought of Hank, she smiled. "He's seven."

"Good boy?"

"The best."

"Shame you don't have a man for him. Every boy needs a man in his life."

She leaned forward. "Excuse me?"

"It's true," Mr. Riddell said, all bluster. "Boys need men to show them how to get on in the world." He turned to Cal, who'd been clenching his teeth next to her. "Don't you think so, Junior?"

"I think Susan's boy is no interest of ours."

As Rosa continued to shuffle, Cal's dad crossed his arms over his chest. "Or maybe you do have a man? Junior said the two of y'all have become close." Looking her up and down, he murmured, "How close are y'all?"

Susan sputtered, "Not very. We just met."

Right in front of her eyes, Cal looked embarrassed as could be. "Dad—"

"Don't fuss. I'm just askin', Junior."

Rosa clucked. "Cal, enough." Far more kindly, she said, "Susan, why don't you pull up that chair and join us for another round of cards." Her eyes lit up. "Hey, we could play poker."

Suddenly, Mr. Riddell looked as handsome as his son. "Rosa, that's the best thing I've heard all day. It's about time you said something worthwhile."

Holding the deck in between her palms like a Vegas dealer, she said, "Texas Hold'em?"

"I'm sorry. I can't stay here much longer," Susan said. "I'll have to pass."

Warily, she looked Cal's way. To her astonishment, he got to his feet, as well. "I'm going to need to leave soon, too." Cal looked her over. "By the way, how's your day been?"

"Great right now. Being with residents is the favorite part of my day."

"She works hard," Rosa told Cal Sr. "Sometimes too hard, I think."

Mr. Riddell glanced at her. "You could use some color on your skin. What you need, missy, is some time out in the sun."

"Maybe this weekend," she said. No way was she going to tell these Texans that she couldn't take the September heat.

"Junior, has Susan been out to the ranch?"

"No, sir."

Susan might have been mistaken, but she could have sworn his eyes twinkled with amusement.

"You ought to invite her," his dad barked. "Take her on a walk out in the fields. Show her the horses. Better yet, take her for a ride. Do you ride, Susan?"

"Bikes. Not horses."

"It's time you took a horse out for a spin, then. Junior, you need to teach her that."

Just imagining how embarrassed she'd be, attempting to ride next to him, made her shake her head. "Really, I don't think so."

"Horseback riding is good exercise," Mr. Riddell practically growled. "You have a problem with that?"

"Oh, brother," Rosa murmured.

"Not at all."

"Good. Now, riding horses is good for your soul. You best make plans to do that, and soon."

Darting a look Cal's way, she noticed he was looking just about anywhere but at her. Now feeling terribly awkward, she edged away. "It really is time I went. I need to check on a few more things...."

Cal turned to his father in obvious exasperation. "I can get my own dates, Dad."

"Not very well."

Susan attempted to give Cal a way out. "That's a very nice offer, but I'm afraid I couldn't accept, anyway. I don't ever leave Hank to go on dates."

"Well, shoot. That's easily solved. Bring your boy along," Mr. Riddell boomed. "He's going to love the ranch." Nudging Cal, he said, "I can't do no more for you."

"Susan, would you care to come over to our ranch this evening?" Cal asked stiffly. "With your boy, of course."

She knew he was embarrassed. So was she. She knew he was only asking out of obligation. She got that.

"Thank you, but it's just not a good idea. I really better continue on my rounds."

Cal frowned. "Wait—I'll walk out with you. Dad, I'd better head on home, now that we might have company coming over and everything."

"I'll see you tomorrow, then?"

Susan couldn't help but notice that there was a new note of hope in Calvin Sr.'s voice.

She noticed that Cal noticed it, too. His eyes softened for a moment and all the love she'd suspected he kept bottled up tight inside him flashed brightly. Then he schooled himself again. "Sure, Dad, I'll see you tomorrow." Tipping his hat, he nodded to Rosa. "Ma'am."

Rosa waggled her fingers. "See you soon, Junior."

After a few more goodbyes were shared, he walked by her side. "So, are you really going to turn me down?"

"You mean, turn *your father* down? He's the one who pushed this."

"Even so, it might be fun. Hank could see the horses. And meet Ginny."

"Ginny will be there?"

"Yeah. She's a year younger than Hank, and a girl, but she's good company. They might have fun."

Oh, she knew Hank would love it.

Thinking about a Friday night with nothing planned, she asked, "Do you mind if I really do take you up on your offer? It would be a treat to see your ranch."

"Actually, I was just about to ask you the same thing. I, uh, would like to see you again. And Hank." He looked at his boots. "I was about to ask if y'all wanted to go out for pizza or something. Having y'all at the ranch sounds real good, too." Lowering his voice, he added, "There's something about that boy of yours I like."

And just like that, all her reasons for ignoring him vanished. Hank was her vulnerable spot. She was willing to do most anything to make him happy. "All right. Around four?"

"Four's good." He paused, then took her hand. "Sue, I'm glad you're coming over."

His hand was callused and hard, just like a man. But he

was clasping her hand so gently, Susan realized that there was a softness inside him, too. "I…I am, too."

Then he turned and walked away before she could say anything else. In fact, she stood there a good long minute. All the while thinking that *Sue* sounded really nice on his lips.

Chapter Nine

This was most likely one of her worst ideas ever. But as she drove down the narrow two-lane highway to the Riddell Ranch, Susan had to admit that all her worries had little to do with Hank's happiness and a whole lot more to do with the way Cal made her feel.

From the backseat, it was evident that Hank had no worries at all. "What's Ginny like, Mom?"

"I don't know. I told you, all I know is that she's a year younger than you."

"What if I don't like her?"

"Then I guess you won't."

A herd of cattle appeared on their left, the small cluster of brown and white making her smile.

"Mom, what if I start to feel bad?"

She gripped her steering wheel harder. Obviously his diabetes was on his mind more than he let on. Softly, she said, "If you start to feel bad, you tell me. I've got candy and a shot, too, if you feel real bad. Okay?"

"Uh-huh."

She was about to ask him what kind of answer that was, when she saw the reason for his distraction; they were now driving along an endless line of white posts. The posts signaling to one and all that they were near the Riddell Ranch.

"Wow," Hank said.

Wow was right.

"Do you think we're going to ride horses or just see 'em?" Hank asked as they drove along, the pastureland in her peripheral vision so pristine and inviting, Susan was tempted to take her eyes off the road and stare.

Instead, she focused on her boy's question. "I think we'll just look at them."

"Why can't we go riding?"

She waited to answer him in order to pass a rickety truck piled high with hay bales. "Well, because going riding takes a lot of time, I imagine," she murmured when the truck faded into the distance. "And we're just going to stay for a short visit."

"Oh."

"Don't be sad. I do imagine we'll get to see their horses. A woman at work told me that the Riddells have lots of horses."

"Lots?"

"Uh-huh." A dozen, to be exact. Actually, ever since she'd told Paula that she'd been invited to the ranch, a whole lot of people at the home had started talking to her about the Riddells. And Cal, aka Junior.

As Hank chattered in the backseat, half counting fence posts, they finally came upon the wide, super impressive entrance to the ranch. Slowing down, she turned right, on to the property, and drove through a pair of enormous gates that stood wide open.

As if everyone there was waiting for them.

She and Hank chuckled as the car bounced over the cattle guard. And looked in awe at the majestic wrought-iron sign that arched above them. Made up of a pair of bold black *R*s, she felt as though she was entering a movie set.

Behind her, Hank craned his neck out the window. "Where's their house?"

"I don't know." All she could see were rows of white fences and six brown-and-white cows lazily eating grass.

"What should we do?"

"I guess we'll just keep driving up this road until we see something," she murmured. Staying nice and slow, she pressed the accelerator and slowly started forward. "This is sure pretty, isn't it? Did you see the bluebonnets?"

"The blue flowers? Yeah."

"I think they're pretty. Why, that field almost looks purple, there're so many."

"They're all right."

As the road continued for at least a mile, she prattled on some more, hoping that Hank would think she was simply in a talkative mood. Not that she was feeling nervous. Though everyone and their sister had told her that the Riddells were a big deal, nothing compared to actually seeing the huge spread with her own eyes.

"There's the house!" Hank cried out excitedly.

Ah. Yes. There it was. A huge mansion of a house, all decked out in white, with white columns, to boot. Beyond it was a well-tended barn made of metal and wood and looking for all the world like something out of *Town & Country* magazine. If it all had been built to intimidate unsuspecting visitors, they had done a good job.

She was intimidated. And, okay, impressed. This place was way more than she had ever imagined when Betsy had told her about the famed Riddell mansion.

It was far grander, far more than she'd dreamed it would be…and she had a good imagination. The fact of the matter was, she was gaping at everything just like Hank. "Look over there," he said, pointing to a swimming pool with not one but two diving boards. "Have you ever seen a pool like that?"

"Never."

"And look over there! There's a train car!"

She craned her neck and saw, sure enough, a bright red old-fashioned-looking caboose sitting off to the side. She wasn't sure, but she thought it was serving as a bar or a dressing area for folks who were using the pool. "It sure is fancy, isn't it?" she said with false brightness.

Inside, all she really wanted to do was escape. During all their conversations, she'd always felt as if she and Cal were equals. Now she felt a little less than that.

Actually, she felt as though she'd just stepped off a merry-go-round and into another world. Only, this one was a whole lot nicer and better than any world she'd ever known.

That wouldn't do. She was smart, and she was fine. She really did not need to be intimidated by so much excess. The thing to do would be to visit a bit with Cal, show Hank around…and then get out of Dodge.

"Well, let's get this over with," she murmured, then immediately regretted her words. Once again, she was looking at the negatives instead of the positives.

Cal had been awfully nice, inviting her over as he had.

She needed to show some of the good manners she'd been lecturing Hank about.

Slowly, she turned to the right, then went ahead and parked in the circular driveway in front of the main entrance of the house.

The minute the ignition was stopped, Hank had his seat belt off and his door open. "Good thing I've got my boots on," he said with a wide grin. "Now I fit right in." Scrambling out, he looked her way. "Come on, Mom."

"I'm coming. Settle down, now."

But as she followed him, she couldn't help but feel a pit in her stomach as she contemplated her son's hopeful words. Because, the truth of the matter was, they didn't fit in at all. Not even a little bit.

They weren't ranchers, they weren't rich and she didn't know a soul who'd ever even thought about putting a train car on their property.

At this moment, Cal had all the pluses, and she was a multitude of minuses.

"Well, Hank. Go ring the bell."

But before he even reached the four steps leading up to the beautifully carved door, it opened.

"You made it," Cal said. "I'm glad."

Hank nodded, his face all smiles. "I like your place. Most especially your pool."

Crossing his arms over his chest, Cal laughed. "You'll have to come back and swim when it's a little warmer."

"Oh, I will," Hank said, chattering away. "I bet you swim all the time."

"Hardly ever."

"I love to swim."

She shook her head. "Henry, give Mr. Riddell a moment to get a word in edgewise." Stung, Hank closed his mouth.

As she walked slowly forward, she noticed that Cal had put on a fresh, crisp white button-down shirt and that he must have showered, too. The ends of his hair still looked damp. "I'm sorry he's talking your ear off. He's just excited."

Looking Hank's way, he nodded. "I'm glad. And I'm glad you've got your boots on, too."

Pure adulation shone in her boy's eyes. "I wanted to look like I belonged on a ranch."

"Well, you do, buddy. You fit in real good." Stepping

back, he looked Susan's way. She noticed much of the warm tenderness he'd shown her son was absent.

In its place was something far more circumspect. For a moment, she froze, then turned back to Hank. She knew it wasn't a good idea to get to thinking too much about Cal, or their reaction to each other.

Standing there in the doorway, Hank rocked forward on his boots, looking inside as if it was a display window in a fancy store. "Wow!" he said. "Look at all those hats!"

Cal stepped aside so they could enter. "Come on in and look at them yourself," he drawled. "And later, if you want, I'll give you a tour."

Hank stepped right through, walking to the fanciest hat rack Susan had ever seen.

While he counted hats, Susan looked around. It really was as pretty as a postcard. A large spiral staircase reached upward to the second floor. Wood planks covered the entryway. A grandfather clock chimed as if it was welcoming their arrival.

"Wow," Hank whispered again.

That was her sentiment, too. Wow.

"I won't bore you by walking you through the whole place. How about I just show you a couple of rooms here, and then we'll go out to the barn."

"Where the horses are?" Hank asked.

"Yes. Where the horses are," Cal repeated.

Slowly, Susan followed him, looking at the oriental carpets and the antique furniture. The comfortable suede couches and the massive flat-screen television. It was all beautiful and expensive and, for some odd reason...cozy.

She was just admiring the stainless-steel appliances in the kitchen when the back door opened. In came a trim gray-haired lady and a little girl. Immediately her heart melted. The girl was wearing a jumper and sandals. With a ponytail and wide swath of brown bangs, she was ador- able. "Hey, Junior!" she called out with a smile. "Me and Gwen have been running errands."

"I got the dry cleaning dropped off and Ginny and me picked up some movies at the library," the lady said.

"Thanks." Looking toward Susan, he said, "This is Gwen and Virginia."

"I'm Ginny," the girl corrected.

Cal rolled his eyes. "All right. *Ginny,* Gwen, please meet Ms. Susan Young and her son, Hank."

Gwen held out a hand. "Nice to meet you." She smiled, but Susan noticed that she also had a speculative gleam in her eye. "Are you new to Electra?"

"We are. We've only lived here a couple of months."

"Ah."

"It's nice to meet you both," Susan said. "Cal was just showing us around your place. It's really amazing."

"Oh, darlin', you need to get one thing straight." Gwen grinned, making the lines around her eyes deepen. "This is sure as heck not my place. It's all Riddell. I just work here."

"Gwen is like family, though," Cal said quickly. "She's helped us with Ginny since she was born."

Gwen looked at the little girl fondly. "It's been a plea- sure."

Cal looked at his sister. "I'm fixin' to show our company the barn. Want to come?"

Ginny seemed to have eyes only for Hank. "Uh-huh."

When Hank started to squirm, Susan put her hand on his shoulder as a warning. "Do you have a pony, Ginny?"

Eyes wide, she shook her head. "I have a horse named Casper. He's all white."

With a parting smile at Gwen, Susan followed Cal, Hank and Ginny out of the house. Before they even made it to the gravel walkway that led to the barn, their arrangement shifted. Ginny was walking with Hank and talking a mile a minute.

And Cal had slowed his pace to walk by Susan's side.

"If I'd have known Ginny would take to Hank so easily, I would have brought your boy out here the first day we met," he murmured. "I'm kind of enjoying this peace and quiet. Most days, she talks my ear off."

"Hank is the same way. He's an only child, you know, so sometimes I'm afraid he tries too much for attention."

"They're getting along real good now."

"That they are."

Slowly, he turned and looked at her. "I am glad you came out here. It's nice not talking to you with a hundred people around."

Thinking back to their first conversations, Susan said, "I wasn't at my best at the hospital."

Looking more than a little embarrassed, he murmured, "I have to say that I'm not real at ease at the hospital, either. Or at the nursing home, to be honest. I feel guilty, sticking my dad there. I'm afraid it influences the rest of me, too."

Susan knew he wasn't alone in feeling that way. But she certainly hadn't thought he had been rude to her there. "Actually, I thought you seemed almost nice when I saw you at the Lodge."

As she'd hoped, her comment teased a smile from him. "Well, I was trying to be nice…maybe I succeeded."

"Maybe you did." Shyly, she added, "And you've been on good behavior here, too."

His eyes flashed with humor. "Perhaps all we need is just some time to get to know each other, huh?"

Suddenly, she did want that. "Maybe so."

Finally, they were in the barn. Once again she was struck by how beautifully designed things were. "I always imagined barns would be dusty and smelly. This looks amazing in here."

He laughed, but his posture proved that he wasn't immune to the compliment. "We try hard around here to keep things tidy."

"I'll say. It hardly even smells horsey."

She felt warm all over as he gazed at her again with pleasure. "Aw, honey," he drawled. "That's not really what I'd call a compliment. The horses are the best things we've got."

"Junior, come show Hank Rainy," Ginny said.

"Rainy's one of our mares who's fixin' to foal," he explained to Susan as they joined the two kids.

Susan was impressed with how still Ginny was next to the pregnant quarter horse. Her voice was quiet and gentle, and there was real care with how she examined the horse.

After Cal talked to Hank and her some about the horse, they all moved on. Soon, Cal was playing tour guide, telling Hank and Susan all kinds of tidbits about each horse.

To her surprise, each horse seemed to have its own personality. One of the geldings was an easygoing sweetheart. The other one had a bit of a jokester in him. But with all of them, Cal touched the horses with true fondness. It was obvious in his whole body language just how much he loved the animals.

He was patient with the mare who was shy. Casually waiting for her to approach as if he had all the time in the world.

Susan couldn't help but contrast that attitude with the first time they'd met, when he looked like a caged animal at the hospital cafeteria. That day, she would have sworn up and down that he had patience for nobody.

As they walked on, every so often, Ginny would add a detail, or would embellish the story.

Beside her, Hank looked mesmerized—not by the horses as much as by the man beside them. Gone were his constant questions, as a sort of contemplative speculation entered his eyes. With each moment, Hank seemed to be more and more taken with the somewhat taciturn cowboy.

In spite of herself, Susan knew she was beginning to feel that way, too. This was Cal Riddell in his element, and it gave her such a sense of what the man was really like. Here, she could see how at ease he was with his surroundings, and with the horses.

Gone was the overriding sense of dissatisfaction and stress that had always seemed to emanate from him.

When they walked out of the barn and down a path toward a creek, she looked at him and smiled. "This is where you're happiest, isn't it?"

"Here, at home?" He shrugged. "I suppose that's true. But I imagine most folks feel that way, right?"

Not her. She'd never felt so connected with her home. But maybe that was because she'd been a corporate brat, and they'd moved whenever her father got promotions and new job offers. Her wants and needs had never seemed to matter as much as her father's job.

Of course, she suddenly realized that she'd done the same thing. She'd moved Hank for a better job, and he was suffering for it.

That revelation caught her off guard. So much so, she wasn't ready to share, so she sidestepped it. "Sometimes home doesn't always feel like the best place," she compromised.

"Not for you?"

"Not always," she said lightly, skimming over her memories. "Or, maybe not for everyone." Though he didn't look fooled, she smiled, doing her darnedest to pretend that she was speaking in generalizations, not from personal experience.

"Perhaps not," he agreed. "There was a time when this place didn't feel like home, either. Mom only lived here for a little while before she died. I used to walk around the house and wonder why we had it. My dad was mourning and my brothers and I were suffering." He paused and looked away. "Sorry. I don't know why I just told you all that. I don't remember the last time I thought about those days."

"None of us like being reminded about things that are easier to forget."

Whoa! Their conversation had gotten deep and almost painful very quickly. If she didn't do something fast, they were destined to start talking about her past, and that was too hard. "Hey, you know what?" she said brightly. "This barn, it's great."

He raised an eyebrow. "So, that's what we're doing, hmm? Keeping it easy?"

"At least for now."

Luckily, Hank and Ginny's laughter called them to think of other things. "We better keep an eye on them. Left to their own devices, there's no telling what trouble they could get into."

"I shudder to even think about it," she teased.

And when he held his hand out for her to take, she did, feeling warm and happy. And suddenly as if she belonged somewhere. After all.

Chapter Ten

Just minutes after they got home and she told Hank to take a shower, Betsy was at Susan's back door. "I know you just got home," she said without preamble. "But do you have a few minutes? Can I come in?"

Susan wasn't thrilled about her neighbor's appearance. It had been an exhausting day, what with work and the unexpected invitation to the Riddell Ranch. All she really wanted to do was get cleaned up and sip some decaf coffee.

And try to come to terms with what was going on between her and Cal.

But Betsy looked stressed out and worried. Obviously, she was in need of a friend—and she'd definitely been more than that for Susan. "Of course."

"Oh, thank you." Betsy barreled in, looking nothing like her usual freethinking party-girl self. "I'm in a heap of trouble."

"Then you better sit." With a sense of dismay, Susan sat in the easy chair next to her. "What's going on?"

Betsy opened her mouth, then sighed.

It would have made Susan laugh if she wasn't so worried. "Bets, just spit it out."

"I…okay. It's like this. I have another date with Gene."

"Uh-oh." Wariness coursed through her. "Have you told him the truth about yourself yet?"

Betsy winced. "Not exactly." Biting her lip, she ran her fingers through her hair, making it stick up in about a thousand directions. "It's really driving me crazy, if you want to know the truth."

Susan would've smiled if she didn't think Betsy was about to start crying. "Um, I thought we agreed that living honestly was the best thing to do."

Betsy held her hand out like a school crossing guard. "Hold it right there. Living honestly is a whole lot harder to do than just planning to live that way. I had lots of good intentions about telling Gene the truth. But time just got away from me."

"Betsy—" With a strong sense of foreboding, Susan had a terrible feeling that she was about to be talked into yet another thing she didn't want to do.

"No, hear me out. I really had planned to tell Gene that I wasn't quite the woman he thought I was. That I, you know, had been around the block. A time or two."

"Uh-huh?"

"But, Susan, his eyes glowed when they looked at me. Like I was worth his time. Like I was something special." She looked at Susan, and there was such a vulnerability in Betsy's eyes, Susan ached for her—even though she kind of wanted to strangle the girl, too.

"You already are worth his time. And special."

"Honey, I'm not that special. If he knew my complete past, he'd write me off like a tax deduction."

Susan couldn't help it, her lips twitched. "Maybe not that quick."

Betsy was too frazzled to see any humor in her situation or Susan's comment. "With Gene, things are different. See, a funny thing happened on my way to taking advantage of Gene. I began to like him." She darted a look Susan's way. "I like him a lot. It's different, you know, when you have someone look at you like you might be everything they've ever dreamed of." More quietly, she added, "It's different when someone looks at you and you start to feel that way, too."

With a sinking heart, Susan was afraid she knew exactly what Betsy was talking about. That was how she was starting to feel about Cal. That she didn't want to like him, but there was something about him that kindled her interest.

Even though he hardly ever smiled. Even though he was wary about her. Even though he was everything about Texas and roots and she still wasn't even sure if she was going to stay in Electra.

But no matter how hard she tried, she couldn't deny that she thought about him a lot. Had even hoped that there would be more to them than there seemed to be.

Down the hall, Susan heard Hank turn off the shower. In mere minutes, her boy was going to be barreling in, hungry for a snack and ready to talk more about their ranch visit.

The discussion about Betsy's love life was going to have to wrap up soon.

"I feel for you, but you really are going to have to tell him the truth. It absolutely needs to be sooner than later." She stood up, hoping Betsy would take the hint.

But Betsy simply leaned back with a long, dramatic sigh. "Susan, have you ever met a man who wishes you were more than you were? Who makes you wish you could take a really good eraser and just remove certain parts of your past?"

Susan stilled. "Of course I have." She'd felt that way today, when she'd been standing across from Cal Riddell. When he'd looked at her, when he'd talked about dreams… she'd wanted to believe, too. She'd wished for a split second that she hadn't hooked up with a loser and now had to constantly put a small boy's needs first.

Which, of course, was a terrible thing to think about. And was something she could never, ever admit to another soul. Suddenly feeling worn out, she sighed. "I'm sorry, but I'm exhausted. Can we talk about this tomorrow?"

Betsy's eyes popped open. "Actually, I came over for a favor."

Right on cue, the bathroom door opened. "Mom?"

"Hey, honey," she said when Hank padded down the hall in his favorite pajamas. "Betsy's here, but she's just about to leave. Why don't you go put your dirty clothes in the hamper."

"Okay."

As soon as he turned away, Susan said, "Betsy, cut to the chase. What do you need?"

"I need you to go on that double date with me."

"No."

"But Gene has a friend."

Oh, no. As in, no way. "I'm sorry, I'm not interested. Now I really do need to go help Hank get ready for bed."

"Please, Susan?" She held up a hand. "Before you say no again, just listen. This friend of Gene's is supposed to be real nice. And he's a plumber."

Betsy was making that sound like a good thing. "Betsy—"

"Plumbers make a lot of money. And listen, it's just going to be dinner. At the Golden Dove." She paused meaningfully, then continued in a rush. "Susan, you're gonna want to say yes, if only to get a free meal. And this meal is worth dating a plumber for, I promise. It's the best restaurant in town. And, this plumber knows the Riddells. Maybe he could even give you some information about them."

"Why would I want that?"

"If you've got a crush on Cal, you're going to need help.

He's tough to get to know. Believe me, I've tried. So, see? There's a hundred reasons to say yes to this double date."

"I don't think I can get a sitter." This, of course, was true. She didn't know who she could call…and she didn't know how she'd even pay for it. "Plus, I'm not interested. At all." Plus, well, there had been something about the way Betsy had talked about Cal that was disturbing. Just how hard had Betsy tried to get to know Cal?

Betsy paused. "I bet I could find you one."

"Don't."

"This is important, Susan. It's important to me, and you know what, I think it might be important to you, too. You need a night out."

Before Susan could tell her no again, Betsy finally stood up and opened the back door. "Just give me some time to work on this. I'll call you tomorrow," she promised, then three steps later, she disappeared through the hedge.

"Oh, for heaven's sake," Susan murmured as she closed the door and locked it.

Had Betsy always been like this? Thinking she wasn't good enough? Looking for a future with one eye out on the man's income?

"Mom, my clothes are in the hamper," Hank said sleepily as he entered the living room. "But I'm hungry. Can I have some ice cream?"

"Sure," she said, remembering that she still had a carton of sugar-free ice cream in the freezer. "One scoop of strawberry, then it's time for bed. Okay?"

He yawned as he opened a drawer and pulled out a spoon. "Okay."

As she set the bowl in front of him, he took a bite and smiled. "Mom, wasn't that ranch cool?"

"It sure was."

"I liked the horses best."

"I know."

"Mr. Riddell said I could come back and ride one."

"I remember."

He slid another bite into his mouth. "He said I could swim there, too."

"I heard that, as well."

"And that Ginny wasn't so bad."

"She was a sweetheart."

Three more bites cleaned the bowl. After handing her his dish, he looked her in the eye. "Mom, do you like Mr. Riddell?"

"I do." She took care to keep her voice even and light.

Luckily, that was all Hank needed. With a happy smile, he nodded. "Good. I do, too."

Leaning close, she kissed him, then walked to her own bedroom to get ready for her shower.

But moments later, as she stood under the hot spray, she reflected on her last two conversations. It seemed that in spite of herself, she had already made some decisions about Cal Riddell.

One, she liked him. She really, really did.

And two, she wasn't interested in meeting anyone else. No one could measure up to Cal Riddell Jr. Not in her mind.

It was just too bad they didn't have a future. Today in the barn she'd realized that it was time to get her priorities in order. She needed to go back home, and get Hank settled so he was comfortable.

That couldn't be done in a little Texas town.

Nope, she needed to start thinking about making preparations to head back to Cincinnati. For once she was going to put Hank's needs first.

Even if it practically killed her.

Chapter Eleven

"So what did the doctor say?"

"About what you'd expect," Trent said from the other end of the phone. "That crazy bull got the best of me."

Cal drummed his fingers on his desk. As usual, Trent was telling him next to nothing. All his life, he'd done that, treated everyone else's interest as a need-to-know thing. He always had been too cocky for his own good. "Are you going to need more surgery?"

"I don't think so."

"But they're not sure?"

"A lot depends on how the bones heal," his brother replied after a moment. After what felt like a too-long moment. Something was up.

That's when it finally clicked. *Bones.* As in, plural.

This time, Cal didn't even try to fight the impatience that was seeping into his voice. He wanted some answers. Some straight talk. Now. "Bones? Trent, I thought you just broke your arm. This sounds like a whole lot more than that."

"This might be news to you, but there's more than one bone in your arm, Junior."

"I know there's more than one bone. How many did you break?"

"A couple."

"Jeez, Trent. I'm already dealing with Dad and his loco answers. Give me the truth."

"I only broke two. There was a, uh, compound fracture in my forearm."

"Compound fracture?" Even Cal knew that was bad.

"Yeah, but we're good now," Trent said quickly. "My arm's all set up in a god-awful cast and healing. Hurts like crazy, though. Satisfied?"

"Yeah. How are your ribs?"

"Beat up."

"Truth?"

"Three ribs are cracked," Trent admitted after a lengthy pause. "But my concussion's much better," he said, brightening. "And there's no fever. Anymore."

"Anymore?" Cal echoed, feeling a headache of his own coming on.

"And, well, I've got bruises on top of bruises, and I feel like that dadgum bull played volleyball with my backside. But other than that, I'm fine." He paused again. "Now, before you get all prissy on me, let's move on."

"I don't get prissy."

"I called to hear about Dad, not get interrogated by you. Now stop asking me so many questions."

"Someone needs to. Where are you? Are you still in the hospital?"

He sighed. "I am."

People didn't stay in the hospital as long as his brother had unless things were bad. Real bad. "Trent, how about I come out there?"

"Please, don't."

"But I could help you get settled.…"

"Cal, I'm a grown man, not your pimply little brother trailing after you in high school," he said sharply. "It's not like I don't know the risks of trying to last eight seconds on the back of a bull. Odds are good that if I do it enough, sooner or later the bull is going to win."

His brother had a point.

But still, it didn't matter how old he got; in Cal's mind, Trent was fourteen again, wanting to tag along after Jarred and himself but never being able to keep up.

Obviously, things had changed. These days, that drive to succeed was serving him well. "All right," Cal said finally.

"Now, tell me about Dad or I'm going to call over there myself and start being a pain in the ass."

"Dad's at the Electra Lodge and Rehabilitation Center, recuperating."

His voice rose. "You stuck him in a home?"

Cal supposed they could both say things that could be misconstrued. "Dad needs a lot of care, and it's going to take some time to do that. I'm no nurse and, well, we both know he's not going to put up with me taking his blood pressure, let alone giving him advice."

Trent whistled low. "I know that's right. So, how's he doing? Is he behaving himself?"

"More or less. I visited him yesterday. He's doing his best to rile up the old ladies and the nurses there."

"Shoot. He might even be having fun."

"He'd never admit it, but I think he's kind of enjoying all the people there. There's more than enough people to piss off—and not a one of them is a blood relation."

Trent laughed, then inhaled sharply. "Shoot. Don't make me laugh." After he composed himself, he murmured, "Where's Jarred?"

"Steaming it up in some hotel room in Mexico with Serena."

"Call him home and get him to help you out."

"There's nothing he could do that I can't," Cal said,

though in a moment of weakness he had almost picked up the phone.

"You sure about that?"

"Yep. Somebody ought to be enjoying himself right now. Plus, they're due home in a few days. Until then, I've got things under control."

"I bet you do."

A wealth of implication filled Trent's voice. To Cal's dismay, he realized his little brother was once again mistaking his efforts to take care of things as an ego trip. The thought was disappointing. Did the whole family assume he had never wanted anything different?

Or did they never realize he was just trying to do his part?

Feeling perturbed, Cal drummed his fingers on his desk again. "I better get off the phone. I'll call you tomorrow."

"No, I'll call you. I'm hoping they'll spring me, but it might take a while to get settled."

"You going to be okay, recuperating at home?"

That surprised another bark of laughter from his brother. "Hell, Cal. I won't be sitting here by my lonesome! You don't really think I'd refuse some pretty girl's offer of help, do you?"

Now Cal just felt foolish. Obviously he was the only Riddell man who didn't have a steady amount of sex. "Sorry. I don't know what I was thinking. Bye."

When he hung up, he needlessly straightened up the papers on his desk and then went into the main living room of the house.

But it was quiet. Gwen had taken Ginny out to dinner and shopping. Dad was at the home.

It was just him. Sitting alone in their big house that was roomy enough for twenty people. And their families.

A curious sense of isolation slipped over him. Making

him feel a little like a mother suffering from empty-nest syndrome. It felt strange, knowing that everyone else was able to function without him. At the moment, nobody needed him, and he didn't know what to do.

After wandering through the kitchen, he parked himself on the living room sofa and tried to get comfortable. Bored silly, he reached for the remote. Two clicks allowed him to scan the channels. After viewing an array of unfamiliar sitcoms, he flipped to a sports channel. Tried to be interested in the latest football highlights.

But after a good five minutes, Cal clicked off the remote. He'd never had time to watch television in his life, and it didn't look as if he was going to get interested in sitting in front of the tube any time soon.

With a sigh, he poured out two fingers of scotch and escaped the indoors.

CAL BRACED HIMSELF AND went out to his mother's rose garden. The mild late-September weather had kept the flowers blooming, and their fragrance drifted over him.

He gingerly sat on one of the ornate benches his father had had designed after her death. Though he'd seen Jarred out here a time or two, and his father visited the garden at least once a day, Cal always avoided it as much as he could.

The garden was beautiful. The benches were works of art.

But being there brought back such intense memories of his mother, it was almost a physical thing, his reaction to being there.

Plain and simply, being in the garden, smelling the roses—it hurt.

He had never thought to ask Jarred and Trent if the scent of roses reminded them of their mom. Maybe he didn't because he was afraid they'd tell him no and then he'd feel weak.

But even the sight of a rosebud in a vase made memories play in his mind, of how their dad had brought her roses every week during the last year of her life. Cal remembered sitting in the corner of her bedroom when his dad brought in a bouquet. Her eyes had lit up as if that bunch of flowers had been the biggest surprise imaginable.

"Calvin, you spoil me," she'd always said.

And his father had blushed. His father—who never looked rattled by anything life had to offer—had been constantly rattled by her.

And then he had kissed her pale cheek and told her that he didn't spoil her enough.

Cal would've thought he'd have been embarrassed to be there. No one wanted to see their parents all lovey-dovey. Especially not at fourteen. But instead of feeling awkward, his parents' love had made him smile. And feel secure.

Watching his dad try so hard to make her comfortable during her last weeks had meant the world to him.

Unbidden, his eyes watered. He pulled back a sharp sip of scotch and pushed the sad memories away. No good ever came of remembering things that made him sad. There wasn't a thing he could do about the memories or about his feelings of loss that were suddenly hitting him hard in the gut. He knew that.

This was most probably why he never had been one to sit around and stew. All it did was make a man uncomfortable. Or wish for things that weren't.

But still, for just a moment, he ached to see his mother. To hold her hand, and to listen to her voice. Low and melodious and sweet, it had calmed him like nothing else ever had.

And like nothing else ever would. Except maybe the woman he'd seen yesterday. Susan.

Holding her hand while they'd walked had felt nice. And the curious contentment they'd both felt had given him a much-needed feeling of warmth. More and more, he found himself thinking about her. Remembering how pretty those green eyes of hers were.

Thinking about that pretty head of hair of hers. Imagining her in the shower, the long tresses falling heavy against her back and shoulders.

As the scent of roses became too overpowering, he knew he needed something else to think about. Something else to calm him. So, before he talked himself out of it, he stomped back in the house, picked up his cell phone and dialed the number he'd just added last night. After she'd given it to him.

Just in case they'd ever need to talk.

She answered on the first ring. "Cal?"

"Hey." Taking off his hat, he scratched his head, suddenly wondering why he'd thought calling her had been the right thing to do.

"Is everything okay?" she asked, her voice full of concern. "Has something happened with your dad?"

And of course she'd be concerned. It wasn't as though he was in the habit of calling her out of the blue. "No. I mean, nothing new."

"Oh." She waited.

As he heard her pause, he reviewed his incredibly lame responses so far. No wonder he was sitting home alone while his little brother was with more women than he could count.

Fact was, he had no skills where women were concerned.

"Was there…something you wanted?"

"Yes." He swallowed. This was the best he could come up with? When the silence hung on, he struggled to think of something to say. "I, uh, was just wondering how Hank was doing."

"Hank? Oh. Well, he's fine. Actually, he's better than that," she answered, a smile in her voice. "He's at the movies with a boy from his class. Billy's parents invited him."

He remembered how worried she'd been about the boy making friends. "So he's got himself a friend."

"Yes, and I'm almost giddy about it."

So she was alone. Instantly, his body clicked awake as desire hit him hard. However, he did his best to focus on Hank. The, uh, reason he called. "I think I'm almost as happy for you as him, then."

"Thank you. I'll take your happiness. It's hard being the new kid in a small town. And he's missed a lot of school, too. And, the teacher told the class he was a diabetic, so everyone right away labeled him as different."

"You didn't want anyone knowing?"

"No," she said. "It's not that I didn't want anyone knowing, I just didn't want to mark him as different."

"But he is different."

"He has a disease, Cal."

"Well, lots of kids don't, so he is different."

She exhaled loudly. "What I'm trying to say is that it's been a good thing that the other kids know. I mean, it helps when the moms bring in cupcakes and Hank has to pass them up. But it's just another reason he's different, you know? I mean, he already doesn't have a father. He's from up north, too. That's really different for here. And sometimes kids don't want different."

He felt like an idiot. After a pause, he replied, "Sorry. I hadn't thought about those things. I imagine you're right."

Then, "Who's his teacher? I know almost everyone around here. Maybe I could talk to her...."

"Cal, I don't need you to do that. I can talk to my son's teacher if there's a problem."

"Oh. Um, sure you can. I didn't mean that you couldn't."

"You were just trying to take charge?"

"I was just trying to help," he corrected. "It's a bad habit of mine. I can't help but want to manage things."

"To do them yourself."

He felt his cheeks heat. "Pretty much. I'm trying to do better, though. Listen, how about we forget I said anything."

She paused on her end of the line. "No. Listen, I'm sorry. My son is a sensitive subject for me. I've been really wondering if moving here has been the right thing to do. You're only trying to help, and I appreciate that."

He chuckled. "Sue, we can't even apologize to each other without arguing, can we?"

"Sometimes we can get along," she said slowly. "We got along great at your ranch."

They sure had. Walking to the window, he ran a finger along the pane. Checked for nonexistent dust. Gathered his courage. "Susan, when is Hank due home?"

"Not until about ten or so. They're getting ice cream after the movie."

"So, what are you doing?" His fingers played with the slats on a pair of blinds, moving them up and down. Honestly, could he be any more awkward and teenager-like?

She chuckled. "Oh, I'm having a great Saturday night. I'm sitting here looking at a book."

The way she phrased it caught his attention. "Looking?"

"I don't think you can call it reading if I've been looking at the same page for the last hour."

Examining his almost full glass of scotch, he murmured, "Would you like to go get a drink or something?"

"Like at a bar?"

He was tempted to invite himself to her place, but he thought that would be pushing it. Ditto with her coming over to his place, since he was home alone. They weren't teenagers, but he didn't want her to think he wanted more than she could give.

"Yeah. We could go to Bob's, if you'd like."

"The honky-tonk?"

He grinned. The way her voice rose made it sound as if he'd just asked her to meet him in a strip club—not that Electra even had one of those. "It is a honky-tonk, technically, but really it's just a hangout for most of the town. Have you really not been in there?"

"No."

"Picture peanut shells on the floor, a pair of pool tables that have seen better days and a wide assortment of folks from town, all either drinking beer, whiskey or soda. It's not a wild place, by any stretch of the imagination." Well, at least not now, after the Riddell boys had finished sowing their oats. "Well, what do you say? We might as well keep talking, since we're almost getting along and all."

"Can I meet you in the parking lot? I don't want to go in by myself."

"That sounds fine. Or I can pick you up."

"I'm on the other side of town. It's out of your way."

He looked at his watch. It was eight o'clock. "Want to meet in, say, twenty or thirty minutes?"

"Sure. I'll see you then."

When they hung up, Cal felt the warm feeling of satisfaction slide over him.

He refused to contemplate what he was so happy about.

Chapter Twelve

Susan decided to wear a skirt with a thin silk tank top, all in violet. After about two seconds' deliberation, she'd opted out of jeans—most of the girls in town wore Western-cut jeans with sandals or boots.

In contrast, most of Susan's jeans looked too tailored. Momlike.

And, well, if she was going out—finally—she wanted to look nice. So she'd put on a skirt and strappy sandals, figuring that even if she didn't fit in with what the rest of the girls at Bob's were wearing, why, at least she'd feel good about herself.

As soon as she'd gotten off the phone, she'd stared at it as if it were a live thing. Getting a call from Cal Riddell had been unexpected. But it had been a very nice surprise, too. Susan wasn't quite sure why Cal had decided to call her, and she wasn't going to stew over it too much. All she'd known was that she was going to go crazy if she sat and stared at the same page in her book for another hour, feeling guilty about turning down Betsy's offer of the double date.

Oh, Betsy hadn't been too thrilled with her answer when she'd called her that morning. Though she had pushed and prodded, cajoled and bribed…Susan had stayed firm. She wasn't interested in going on a date with Betsy's almost-boyfriend's friend. Especially since she was uncomfortable with Betsy's comment about dating men who had money.

Of course, wasn't that what she was doing now? Getting ready to meet Cal Riddell—just about the richest man in town—at a honky-tonk?

Susan certainly wasn't a saint, but trying to snag a man because of his income certainly wasn't one of her faults.

Plus, she hadn't been completely at fault, anyway. She really didn't have a babysitter.

However, starting at four that afternoon, things had begun to change. So much so, it was as though a fairy godmother had appeared and decided to take things into her own hands. Suddenly Hank had plans, with a boy whose parents Susan had met and trusted.

And then Cal called.

Now, here she was, sitting in Bob's parking lot, watching a whole assortment of folks wander in and out. Every so often—well, every two minutes or so—she craned her neck around, watching for Cal's truck.

Just when she'd begun to worry if he had decided to stand her up, there he was—looking as perfect and handsome as he ever did. His jeans were dark and snug fitting. Around his waist was a finely crafted leather belt, fastened with a silver buckle. The oxford shirt he wore was starched enough to stand up on its own.

The man oozed confidence. He stood near the entrance, glancing around the parking lot. Waiting for her. As she gathered her purse, she saw him nod to a couple of women who walked by, his expression friendly but distant.

She stepped out of her car and locked it. When she straightened again, she saw him walking toward her.

And there was a look of appreciation in his eyes that was unmistakable.

"You made it," he said. "Right on time, too."

"You, too." There was no need for him to know that she'd come early.

"I was afraid I was going to be late. Gwen and Ginny came in as I was leaving. I had to answer a dozen questions about why I was looking so slick on a Saturday night."

Now that she knew Gwen, Susan had a feeling the questions were laced with humor. "Was Gwen glad you were going out?"

"Glad is kind of putting it mildly. She's thought I should get out more for some time."

Looking bored with the talk about himself, he held out a hand. "So, are you ready to get a good look at the best Electra has to offer?"

Hesitantly, she slid her palm in his. It felt warm and callused against her hand. Solid and secure. "I'd be a fool to say no, I think."

"Don't fret. Like I told you on the phone, it's more of a town hangout than anything." He dropped her hand to open the door for her, then guided her through it with a hand on the small of her back.

Immediately, she was enveloped in a cloud of cigarette smoke, the scent of stale beer and the blare of loud music from the jukebox. Even louder was a group of twenty-something men and women in a room off to the side. "That's the game room," Cal said, his fingers still grazing her hip. "The pool tables are in there."

The rest of the bar was made up of roughly ten square wooden tables, a long bar that ran along the back wall and at least thirty more people of assorted ages either sitting or standing in groups.

Almost all of them looked their way. And a good number of them either nodded or said hello to Cal.

And then they gave her a good once-over.

Susan shivered a bit, feeling on display. Cal eyed them

all, as usual not smiling. Though he hardly did more but touch the small of her back, she felt as if he'd just stared everyone down. Telling them without a word that she wasn't available.

She should mind that, yet somehow she didn't.

Instead, she smiled at him as he held a chair out for her, then he sat down beside her.

Soon their server came over.

"Junior," she said with a smile. "Hey."

"Hey there, Jolene," he said to the knockout-gorgeous blonde wearing short shorts and a T-shirt stretched so tight across her chest, that the Bob emblazoned in bright blue letters looked like Boob at first glance.

For the first time all night, Cal smiled. "How you doing? How's that baby of yours?"

"She's perfect and I'm good enough. I haven't seen you in ages. How's your family?"

"We've been better. Dad's in the hospital. Trent is, too."

Something flickered in Jolene's eyes. It was a tactic that Susan knew well. Hiding an interest that would be better hid. "Is he okay?"

"Trent? Yeah. He got thrown off a bull and is wishing for pain relief, but he's hanging in there."

Susan noticed there was an odd gentleness in his voice.

"Thank goodness. And your daddy?"

"He had heart surgery, but he's gonna be okay, too."

Looking Susan's way, he shook his head and dropped the smile. In that now-familiar way that told her he was disappointed in himself. "I'm sorry, Susan. I didn't mean to ignore you. Sue, this is Jolene. We've been friends forever. Jo, this is Susan Young. She works at the Electra Lodge." He winked. "As the director of Human Resources."

"Nice to meet you," Susan said, trying not to dwell on the fact that he had introduced her by her job, not by their relationship. Of course, what were they anyway? Friends? More than that?

Jolene smiled. "It's nice to meet you." Her words were sweetly said.

But Susan noticed the woman was looking her over curiously, obviously trying to figure out where she fit in the scheme of things. Suddenly, Susan realized that she didn't have a single thing in her closet that would have been appropriate for this place.

Shoot. She looked as if she was going to a business meeting, not out to a bar with peanut shells strewn everywhere.

Jolene grabbed the tray she'd pushed over to the side when they'd all started talking. "Well, I'm sure y'all didn't wander in here to visit with me. What can I get you?"

Cal looked her way. "Susan?"

"A light beer?"

"I'll take a Bud."

Jolene winked. "One Bud Light, one Bud coming up."

When she walked away with a swish of her hips, Susan noticed more than one or two cowboys watch her walk. "Wow," Susan said, thinking Hank's word about the ranch seemed the only suitable reaction. "She's pretty."

Looking Jolene's way, he grinned. "That she is."

"You seem close. Did y'all date?"

Under his black Stetson, his eyebrows rose. "No. She's quite a bit younger than me. And, well, since we were small, she was always Trent's friend." He smiled. "She's always had a thing for my brother, if you want to know the truth."

"Was it mutual?" Susan watched Jolene laugh with a couple other women behind the bar, grab two bottles of beer, then approach them again.

"Not as mutual as one of them hoped," he said quickly

as Jolene approached. When she placed an icy-cold bottle in front of each of them, he smiled at the blonde again. "Thanks, Jo. We'll run a tab."

"You got it," she said with a grin before walking toward another couple.

When they were alone again, Cal raised his bottle. "Here's to us, Susan. Here's to going a whole ten minutes without arguing."

She raised her bottle, too. "I'll drink to that. I'm really glad you called. All I was doing was sitting on the couch worrying about Hank."

When she saw a flash of hurt appear in his eyes, she automatically reached out and grabbed his hand. "I didn't mean that how it sounded. I'm thankful you called. And, uh, glad to be here. I promise."

He tipped his beer her way again before taking a sip. "You know what? Right now, I think I'm going to believe you."

The way he looked at her made her feel all girlish.

She sipped her beer, too, and scooted a little closer to him, because it was so noisy it was hard to hear.

Yes, that would have made sense…if they'd been talking, but they weren't.

She was tempted to slide even closer.

If Betsy and her date hadn't walked right in.

Chapter Thirteen

"Shoot," Susan said.

With effort, Cal made himself stop staring at her—he'd never seen a woman with such soft-looking skin—and concentrate on her new tense expression. "What's wrong?"

"That woman who just walked in is my neighbor."

The redhead with the pixie cut looked vaguely familiar. He couldn't quite place her. However, he definitely recognized the man she was with. Gene Howard. Ever since his girlfriend had left him for someone else, Gene had kind of fallen apart. He had a slump in his posture that made him look like a perpetual sad sack. His eyes were brown and his lips were pale enough that they kind of blended in with his skin tone. All in all, he was a mousy man with a pooch hanging over his belly and sallow skin.

"Do you know Gene?" he asked. "Are they serious?"

"I don't know him at all. But, uh, Betsy had wanted me to double-date with her and one of Gene's friends this evening. I told her no."

Cal narrowed his eyes at the girl, then the name Betsy finally triggered a memory. She'd flirted outrageously with Trent a time or two last summer. When Trent hadn't taken her bait, she'd moved on to him. Had even gone so far as to ask him out.

He'd refused her, of course. He didn't like pushy women, and her behavior had given credence to the rumors Trent had told him about. Betsy was a woman desperate for a wedding ring and an easier life. Looking for love had very little to do with her agenda.

In his estimation, Susan didn't seem like the type of woman to keep company with a girl like Betsy.

But just as he was about to ask Susan why she'd told Betsy no, the redhead approached, Gene in tow.

As they got closer, he compared her red hair to Susan's. Where Betsy's was the product of a bottle, he instinctively knew Susan's auburn was the work of nature. That key difference seemed to suit what he knew about each woman, as well. Betsy's pushy fakeness had grated on him. While Susan's personality seemed to illustrate exactly who she was.

Yep, even when he hadn't liked her all that much, Susan hadn't tried to be someone she wasn't.

"Hi, Betsy," Susan said when Betsy and Gene were barely a foot away.

Her friend's eyes flashed. "Well, now, you are about the very last person I would have ever expected to see here." Looking Susan up and down, she added, "You know, you should've just told me you already had plans." As she turned to Cal, she winked slowly. "Hey, Junior."

"Betsy."

Susan gripped her beer bottle. "When we talked earlier, I didn't have plans. Cal and I just decided to go out for a little bit. It was kind of a spur-of-the-moment thing."

"Is that right?" Betsy opened her eyes innocently and scanned the bar. "Now, where's Hank? In the bathroom?"

"You know he's not here."

"How can that be? I mean, you've told me a dozen times

that it was too hard to get a babysitter so you could go out for a night on the town with me."

"Hank is at the movies with a friend."

Cal bit his lip and waited for Susan to tell her friend that why she was here and what Hank was doing was really none of her business. Certainly not any of Gene's.

But Susan seemed uncomfortable and tongue-tied. In contrast, Betsy looked triumphant, which just made him pissed. Already, he couldn't wait to tell her goodbye.

Stepping a little closer, she smiled. "Junior, it really is so good to see you again. Do you know Gene Howard?"

"I do. How you doing, Gene?"

"Fair enough, thanks."

When Betsy didn't introduce Susan to him, Cal did the honors. "Susan, this here is Gene Howard. We've known each other forever."

Smiling weakly, she held out a hand. "It's a pleasure to meet you."

Cal waited, sure the Susan he'd met at the hospital was about to appear. That Susan would've torn into Betsy's know-it-all attitude and asked her to leave them alone.

But instead of doing any of that, Susan slumped in her seat.

So Betsy took charge. "We had a real nice dinner at the Golden Dove. Have you been there, Cal?"

He and Jarred had gotten takeout from there for a good two weeks for their father when he'd had his first episode with his heart. "I have," he said shortly. It irked him that Betsy was now pointedly directing all her attention toward him.

"How's Trent doing? Still raising eyebrows on the circuit?"

"Some." He didn't feel the need to share Trent's recent

misfortune. It wasn't as if Gene—or Betsy—was going to have a reason to give Trent a call anyway.

Betsy crossed her arms in front of her chest as Gene smiled. "Hey, how about I try to find us another pair of chairs? We could make it a foursome."

Confused by Susan's behavior, and in no mood for either Betsy's or Gene's company, Cal decided to put an end to things. "That would be real nice, if we'd wanted company," Cal finally said. "However, we do not."

After tossing Cal a glacial glare, Betsy allowed Gene to guide her out of the way and to a table near the back.

The moment they were out of sight, Susan exhaled and relaxed against him. "I'm sorry I just sat here like a statue," she whispered. "Seeing her really shocked me."

He couldn't deny that he didn't mind her sidled up against him at all. In fact, he almost welcomed Betsy's interruption. For the first time, Susan was able to let down her guard. As if he did it all the time, he carefully slipped an arm around her shoulders and held her close. "If you don't mind me saying so, she didn't look all that happy to see you, either."

She chuckled but didn't move away. "Oh, she wasn't."

Behind them, the band was setting up. Pretty soon the noise was going to be so loud that no one was going to be able to say much at all. Because Susan looked so upset, he asked quickly, "Want to tell me what that was all about?"

"Betsy's mad that I didn't want to double-date with her tonight. But back when she asked, I honestly couldn't go. And, well, I didn't want to, either."

Because they were close enough to kiss, he noticed little flecks of gold and violet around the edges of her green eyes.

"Because?" he murmured.

"Because I don't date, Cal. You know that by now, right? I can't afford it, and I can't afford to leave Hank in some-one else's hands for very long. His diabetes is too new to me to trust him with a teenager. It's only because he's with his buddy's family that I said yes to you."

"So you told her all that and she understood?"

"I told her all that and she didn't understand even a little bit," she corrected. "This guy's important to her."

"So is his bank account," he said drily. "Susan, I know she's your friend and all, but I should probably warn you that she doesn't have the best reputation. About a year ago, she tried hard to get her claws into Trent. Luckily, he wasn't looking for anything long-term."

With a sigh, she moved away from him. "I don't agree with her motives, but other than that, I really have liked her a lot." Susan bit her lip. "She's come over and we've sipped wine and laughed. She looked so mad at me, I wonder if she'll even talk to me tomorrow."

"She will. When she wants something from you she will."

"That's not fair."

"Lots of things aren't fair." He felt for her. He knew she'd taken on a lot, and now that he was getting to know her better, he knew how hard she worked. Just for a moment, he'd been anxious to see the lines around her eyes relax. Lessen. And, of course, he'd been enjoying having his arm around her. Dressed in that violet tank top, her skin was as supple and smooth as he'd imagined.

He'd enjoyed feeling as if she needed him, needed his support. Just for a little while.

But maybe it wasn't too late? "Hey, want to get out of here?"

Her eyes lit up. "Can we?" Then just as quickly, she

caught herself. "Oh, I mean, it's okay. I don't want to make you leave."

He laughed. "We can do whatever we want. So, answer me, would you? Do you want to leave?"

"I'd love to, if you don't mind." Worry appeared in her eyes. His heart softened. Susan didn't want to disappoint him. She was putting his needs first. Right then and there, he realized that she would sit at their table at Bob's for as long as he wanted, if it was going to make him happy.

Even if her neighbor was shooting arrows at her from her perch on Gene Howard's lap.

Who else had ever put him first? He couldn't think of a situation recently where his preferences had even been acknowledged. Susan's thoughtfulness made him wistful for things that he'd given up on. And it humbled him, too.

"Let me settle up and then we'll go," he said softly.

"You really don't mind?"

"Not at all, sweetheart."

Surprise at his endearment made her eyes widen. Well, that made two of them. He didn't call women sweet little names.

But what struck him as even more surprising was her reaction.

She obviously wasn't used to hearing sweet things. Why not? he wondered. Had no one ever cared enough to treat her sweetly?

BY MUTUAL AGREEMENT, they left her car in the parking lot at Bob's and headed out in his truck.

"Where we're going is close," he murmured. "Not more than ten minutes away."

"I'm learning ten minutes is close in Texas."

He chuckled. "Well, darlin', everything is big here," he said in an exaggerated drawl.

As he'd hoped, it earned a chuckle from her. And a smile when he reached for her hand.

As promised, he was parking in no time at all. "This ain't the honky-tonk," he said as they started down the sidewalk. "But I always thought our town square had a certain charm," he murmured as he held out his arm for her to take.

"I would agree." Susan realized, to her amazement, that she hadn't been out in Electra much at night. The Lodge was on the outskirts, in between the hospital and her condo. Because of that, she hadn't had the opportunity to experience the true prettiness of Electra in the moonlight.

The town leaders had strung lights through most of the trees in the center square. The surrounding buildings, while looking old and in need of a serious paint job in the daylight, looked adorable festooned with tiny white lights. Still more tiny lights dotted potted plants and shrubs along the walkway. It all looked magical.

"I had no idea everything was lit up like this," she murmured. "I'm glad you brought me here."

"That's good."

And because she was starting to get the idea that Cal did thoughtful things all the time, with no expectation of ever receiving thanks, she added, "I'm glad you called me up, too, Cal. Thank you."

His hand tightened around hers for a split second before he answered, "Watch out, Sue. If you're not careful, you're going to stop being irritated with me. Next thing you know, you'll be sitting at home, waiting by the phone, hoping I'll call."

"I better be extra careful, then," she joked. "I'll hardly know what to do with myself then."

"Would that be so terrible?" There was the faintest hitch in his voice. In the dim light she wasn't sure if he was still teasing her...or if he'd become more serious.

"If I was reduced to sitting by the phone?"

"If we started getting along?"

"Of course not." As Susan looked up at Cal, gazed into his eyes, she smelled his soap and cologne. A stab of dismay coursed through her.

Because right then and there, she knew that she did want to get along with him. She was even forgetting why she had never got along with him in the first place. Now all she seemed to do was think about how handsome he was. Admire that slow, sexy drawl.

And wonder if he was ever going to kiss her.

But stewing on all that wouldn't do. So she kept things as light as she dared. "For the record, I haven't been trying not to get along with you. I don't know what happened...."

"Maybe we were just at our worst at the hospital."

Cal was giving her an easy way out. It would be so easy to take it. To not accept any blame for her actions. But could she really do that? "Maybe it was the hospital environment," she said slowly. "Or, maybe it's just the time of my life. Things are complicated with me right now. I get stressed and forget that the rest of the world isn't that way, too."

"Because of the move?" He glanced at her with a soft smile, then moved them off to the side as a pair of teenage girls darted by, the two of them giggling while one texted on her cell phone. For a brief moment, Susan's side was flush up against his, her breast pressing into his biceps, her hip against his.

Without notice, a new pulse of awareness zipped between them. With effort, she concentrated on his question. "Yes, I've been feeling at loose ends because of the move. And the job. And Hank's diabetes. He's had so much trouble getting adjusted, I sometimes wonder if I should go back."

"You'd do that?"

"Maybe. It's been a tough adjustment in a lot of ways." She lowered her voice, dismayed that she could still feel as if Hank's illness was somehow her fault. "But that's not the whole reason I've felt so confused."

"Most people would say it was enough."

Susan liked how Cal didn't rush, didn't push her into admitting more than she wanted to. "Most people would be right," she said. Then, slowly, she took the plunge. "But, well, I think the problem was you."

He looked taken aback. "Me?"

She tightened her hand on his arm when he threatened to pull it away. "Yes—but not in the way you're thinking," she said. "Cal, you're the first man since Hank's father who's had any interest for me."

"Why do you think that is?"

"Because before you, I was too afraid. Greg, he hurt me deeply. I can't tell you what that felt like, knowing he not only was rejecting me, but rejecting our baby, too."

"That was his fault, Susan." His voice matched his glare. Both were harsh.

"I know. And I can't say I'm upset about him not being in my life. But it also made me think that the only way to be safe was to push everyone else away. That's what I hate most about what Greg did to me. He made me afraid to ever let anyone get close."

"But with me you're starting to think differently?"

"Yes. I don't know why."

"You don't know. Hmm…" In the reflection of the twinkling lights, his eyes glowed. "Is that a fact?"

His accent had thickened. She was starting to learn that

his voice thickened, became almost more Texan in times of deep emotion. When he was at the hospital. When he discussed getting his father into the Lodge.

And now. When he was about to kiss her.

With sure steps, he led them to the shadow of the bank. Where it was dark, out of the way.

And then, before she knew what to say, he lowered his mouth, cupped her jaw in his hand and kissed her.

Deliberately. Slowly. The same way he seemed to do everything else. With thought and extreme care. A probe of his tongue opened her lips. Then, still holding her face tenderly in his hands, he explored her mouth.

It was the most passionate, heartfelt kiss she'd ever had. His touch, his scent, his taste grabbed her senses and held on tight, making her aware of only him.

Making her hope things would never end.

Slowly, Susan raised her hands and flattened her palms on his chest, felt his heartbeat and kissed him back.

Only after an eternity did he step back.

Only after they gazed at each other in wonder, panting, attempting to get their breath back, did she realize that they were still in the shadows of the building.

And that anyone could have been watching them.

But even more surprising, Susan realized she didn't care.

No, far from worrying about what people thought, only Cal Riddell occupied her mind. Her palms still flat against his cotton shirt, she felt the heat radiate from his skin. As the beat of his heart thumped under her hand, she imagined what he'd feel like without that shirt on.

Okay. Without a stitch of clothing on. She wondered what he'd be like in bed. Would he still kiss her so deliberately?

Would his hands be as methodical and deliberate?

Would he say her name, all soft and slow, emphasizing the first syllable, letting the second drift off into almost nothing?

Even thinking about him, over her, his body naked, his skin bronzed, those grayish-blue eyes of his flashing passion, made her toes curl.

"Maybe…maybe we should walk on," she said softly.

Taking her hand again, he nodded. "Which way do you want to go?"

They were at the street corner. Electra, being the small town that it was, had ended abruptly, with the one stoplight, and was now twinkling in its glory behind them. "What are the choices?"

"Well, Sue, we can turn around and go back the way we came," he drawled. "Or we can make a turn."

"Is there anything of interest in that direction?"

"More than you might imagine. But perhaps, not as much as you might hope."

Susan couldn't help it, she laughed. "Are we still talking about walking?"

"I'm not even sure anymore."

What did that mean?

She was tempted to ask, but when she glanced his way again, he stared only straight ahead. Yet, with his right arm, he covered her hand that clutched his left arm. Gently tracing a finger over the veins in her hand, he caressed it gently before guiding her hand down to join his.

It was a lot of fuss to switch hand positions. But because it had felt so deliberate, every sense was focused only on him.

And she knew if he pushed her up against the wall of one of the buildings, she'd kiss him again. And if he asked her to his bed, why, she'd probably go.

Which all seemed a little too fast.

"Maybe we should go back the way we came," she finally said.

"It's probably the right decision," Cal said after a pause.

She bit her lip. "But maybe next time—if you want there to be a next time—we could try making that turn?"

"Oh, there will definitely be a next time, Susan. And then, I promise, I'll do whatever you want."

Chapter Fourteen

I'll do whatever you want.

All night, those words had reverberated through Susan's head. Cal had sounded so serious. So determined.

And though she was all about being independent and not needing anyone...well, his words had filtered through that almost-tough exterior and reached all her soft emotions.

The tender, feminine feelings she'd done her best to pack away after Greg had broken her heart.

Yep, as soon as Cal had said those words, she'd looked up at him and felt a hard punch of fierce longing. It had thrown her for a loop—after all, she sure hadn't felt desire like that in a very long time.

The fact was, his words had sounded so completely romantic, they'd pretty much taken her breath away. From the time she was a little girl, all she'd wanted was to be loved and appreciated. That had been both a gift and trouble for her. She'd been an overachiever, just to get that gold star from her teacher and smiles from her parents. She'd dated guys because they'd liked her—hoping that eventually she'd return their feelings.

Then Greg had happened.

Her relationship with Greg had been the epitome of that way of thinking. She'd dated him because he'd really liked her, slept with him because she'd hoped she loved him and then had watched everything in their relationship disintegrate into what it actually was the moment she became pregnant. Nothing more than something superficial.

Because of that experience, she'd built up walls around herself. Within those walls, she could be safe. Of course, it had also felt lonely and a bit confining.

Until now.

Cal treated her differently. Though he wasn't one for flowery words or effusive compliments, Susan knew he looked at her in appreciation. In addition, he seemed to enjoy the sparks that flew between them as much as she did. Well, as much as a man like him would allow himself to.

He seemed to almost welcome the moments when they didn't agree. Those cool blue-gray eyes of his would heat up and a hint of a smile could be heard in his voice.

What's more, her hesitance to pursue him didn't turn him cold, either. Actually, her wariness only seemed to make him comfortable.…

And she couldn't deny his kisses had ignited something deep inside her. Rarely had she felt so protected and vulnerable as when he'd carefully placed both his hands on her face and held her to him as he'd kissed her.

His strong demeanor, mixed with his gentle mouth, had triggered a reaction from her she hadn't dreamed possible.

Greg, in comparison, seemed weak in every way. From the way he'd eagerly kissed her…to the way he'd made love to her, hastily and with no thought to her needs…to the way he'd left when life had become too demanding.

And she, like a fool, had taken much of his rejection as her fault. Figuring that once again, she hadn't been good enough to deserve to be loved unconditionally.

Susan had a feeling Cal would never treat her like that.

"Mom? Are you ever going to get out of bed?" Hank called from the kitchen.

With a start, she realized the television was on, and that Hank had already gotten himself up and was having breakfast. "I am, honey," she said. "Are you doing okay?"

"Uh-huh."

Susan slipped on her robe as she padded out to see him. Ruffling his hair, she kissed his brow. "What a good boy you are, getting breakfast on your own." Noticing that he was eating cornflakes with a sugar substitute, she added, "You're even using the right kind of sweetener."

He rolled his eyes. "I told you I'm getting smarter," he said around a mouthful of cereal.

"Yes, you are." Desperate for coffee, she poured grinds into the top of the pot, then started filling the carafe with water. "We've got a whole Sunday with nothing planned. What should we do?"

"I want to go back to the ranch."

Ranch equaled Cal. Which equaled that swirl of desire in her belly. Carefully, she stomped that down. "Oh, Hank. We can't go over there anytime we want. We have to wait for an invitation."

"You think we can get one of those soon?"

Hank was talking like she could pick up an invite at the Piggly Wiggly. "No. We have to wait until it's his idea."

"Can't you call up Mr. Riddell?"

"No, I cannot." She wasn't emotionally ready to see him again. She felt too vulnerable.

Hank slumped. "Well, if we don't get to go to the ranch, what are we going to do?"

After pouring herself a mug of coffee, she sat next to him. "All kinds of things. We have this place to clean, and laundry to do."

Hank made a gagging noise.

"Ha, ha. Just because we don't want to do something doesn't mean we don't have to do it. Now, we both had fun last night, so this morning means we need to do our chores."

In the middle of nodding, Hank stilled. "What did you do last night?"

"I, uh, went out with Mr. Riddell." When Hank's eyes went wide, then narrowed, she rushed to explain. "It was a spur-of-the-moment thing. We just went to a restaurant and then for a walk."

"I wish I could have come, too."

"It was a grown-up time." Standing, she picked up his empty bowl. "Now, go get dressed, and bring me your laundry. We're going to get to work." When he looked to argue, she hardened her voice. "Scoot."

AFTER TWO HOURS OF DOING laundry and cleaning bathrooms next to a sulky Hank, Susan began to wish she had called up Cal and invited themselves over. Anything would be better than cleaning the shower and toilet with a seven-year-old.

"Knock, knock!" Betsy called out from the back door. "Susan? Hank? Y'all decent?"

"Hey, Betsy!" Hank ran out of the bathroom to see their neighbor.

"Hey to you, too. How are you?"

"Not so good. I've gotta help Mom clean this morning."

"Boy, howdy. That is too bad. Were you cleaning all last night, too?"

"No! I went to a friend's!" Susan heard him tell Betsy all about his movie date and their visit to the ranch, and she tried real hard to compose herself. Without a doubt, Betsy had come over to give her grief.

With a pasted-on smile, she joined them. "Good morning," she said.

"Good mornin' to you, too." Betsy, as usual, had her hair perfect, her makeup on, and was wearing a cute little sundress.

All of it was the exact opposite of Susan's tied-back hair, unwashed face and old shorts and T-shirt. "We've been cleaning," she said by way of explanation.

"Cleaning forever," Hank added.

"Susan, do you have a moment to talk?"

"Um, sure. Hank, you want to go take a break?" Hank left without saying a word, obviously worried she was going to give him a chore to do any second.

When he was in his room, Susan pointed to the patio. "Want to sit outside? There's some privacy."

"Sure." As soon as they were on the other side of the sliding glass door, Betsy crossed her arms in front of herself. "I owe you an apology."

That was the complete last thing Susan had thought she'd hear. "Really?"

"Really. Gene and I talked last night, after you left." Looking a bit embarrassed, she said, "Actually, he read me the riot act and I listened. For the record, Gene said he couldn't believe I'd been so rude to one of my best friends."

"He said that?" Susan didn't know if she was more surprised by Gene's words, or the fact that Betsy thought they were that close.

"He did." Taking a seat, Betsy stretched her lean, tan legs out in front of her. "He wasn't real impressed that I was in such a snit 'cause I didn't get my way."

"Did you two have fun? I mean, all things considered?"

"We did. Susan, here's the thing. I started dating Gene because he had money. You know how I've been wanting a man like that."

"I know."

"But, even though I've been on the lookout for financial security and all, somehow it's all taken a backseat to happiness. I just started being happy in Gene's company instead of being happy 'cause he could give me what I want."

"Really?" Now, this was getting interesting.

Betsy nodded. "Uh-huh. He's a good man. Decent. And he's got a sweet way about him that I really like. He's patient. And smart, too. I like that in a man."

Thinking about Cal, and how he managed his whole family's finances, Susan knew she had to agree. "Being smart is a huge plus."

"So are good friends. I don't know what is between you and Cal, and maybe I don't even need to know. But you are really a nice person, Susan." Biting her lip, she added, "Obviously I have a lot to learn about being nice right back."

Susan was in no hurry to discuss Betsy's faults—or her own—again. "Don't worry about it. All this was just a misunderstanding." She was about to ask Betsy if she wanted to go out to lunch with her and Hank, when the phone rang. "I better go get that."

Betsy gave her a wave. "I've got things to do, too. Just, thanks, Susan. Thanks a lot."

Hank got to the phone before she did. As she approached him, she watched her boy's expression go from bored to energized in ten seconds as he jabbered into the phone.

As of late, there was only one person who made him light up like that. "Hank, is that Mr. Riddell?" she whispered.

"Uh-huh. He's asking if we want to go riding. I said yes. Can we?"

Hank's eyes were so bright, Susan knew she'd never be able to say no to the invitation.

Even if being back in Cal's company wasn't something she was prepared for. "Hand me the phone and let me get the full story," she said.

As soon as the receiver was at her ear, she heard Cal's wonderful, gravelly laugh. "Sometimes I think that boy of yours would get excited about the sun shining."

No, he got excited about Cal.

But telling him that was much too revealing. "He's a pretty happy person," she murmured. "Now, could you fill me in?"

"It's nothing big. I was talking to Ginny and she thought maybe Hank would have fun coming out here. I know I'd appreciate his company."

Susan noticed he didn't say a word about hers. "Oh. Oh, yes, Hank would love to play with Ginny. And get a riding lesson."

"Maybe you could stay, too?"

"Of course." That would be the best thing, anyway. In case Hank had an episode. "What time would be good?"

"How about noon?"

"We'll be there. Can I bring lunch?"

After a pause, he said, "That would be real nice. Thank you."

When she hung up, she turned to Hank and sighed. "Well, Henry Young, you got your wish."

He didn't even try to look contrite. "I know."

"Will you promise to be a good boy and listen when Mr. Riddell teaches you how to ride?"

"I promise."

She wrapped an arm around his shoulders. "Then we have things to do. We have laundry to finish and lunch to make. Get ready to move like lightning."

Hank laughed as he ran to the dryer and started pulling

out clothes. Susan followed behind, thinking she wasn't fooling herself one bit.

She hadn't agreed for Hank's sake.

She'd agreed to the invitation because she wanted to see Cal again. Badly.

ALL AFTERNOON, SUSAN had watched Hank and Cal with a lump in her throat. Moments after they'd pulled up to the Riddells' home, Ginny had run out of the house and practically pulled Hank to the barn.

Cal had waited for Susan, then carried her canvas tote bag into the kitchen, where she'd put the sandwiches and potato salad in the refrigerator.

Moments later, the riding lesson had begun.

Hank had looked nervous, sitting on top of that horse, but his nervousness hadn't seemed to bother either Cal or the horse much at all.

Quietly, Cal had talked to Hank about the parts of a saddle and bridle, then gave him pointers on his posture. Only then had Cal taken the lead rope and slowly led Hank around the corral.

"He's doing real good," Ginny told Susan when she stood on the bottom rung of the iron fence that made up the corral.

Hank did look good. Actually, he looked as if he was having the time of his life. "Your brother looks like he's a good teacher. Did he teach you to ride?"

"Oh, no. Daddy did." Her chin rose a bit. "Daddy used to ride in the rodeo, you know."

Susan had definitely not known that. But before she could comment, Ginny continued. "But Junior's the one to go to if you need help with something."

"Is that right?"

"Uh-huh. Jarred gives hugs and reads me stories. Trent

plays games and makes me laugh. But Junior's the one to go to if you need help."

Unbidden, a lump formed in Susan's throat. What would it be like to have someone so steady and dependable in her life? "I think everyone needs someone like that. Someone who will always be there for you."

Ginny nodded. "Gwen says that's why Junior's the one here helping Daddy so much. Even if he wanted to do something else, he wouldn't."

Susan tore her eyes from Hank's lesson and studied Ginny with a smile. She was intrigued by the dynamics of the family. "I have a feeling you're right," she murmured. "I don't think Cal could walk away from a responsibility even if it bit him."

Ginny giggled. "I don't think Daddy's bitten Cal yet. But he might."

After the lesson, they ate in the kitchen. When Ginny took Hank out to see the inside of the caboose, Susan smiled Cal's way. "Have I thanked you for today?"

His eyes warmed. "Only about a dozen times. It's not necessary, Susan. We wanted to see you and your boy."

"I think Hank loves horseback riding."

"That's a good thing. At least around here, it is. Riding is just part of who we are." Reaching out, he took her hand and pulled her closer. "Next time y'all come out here, you need to get on the back of a horse, too."

Two steps brought her flush against his chest. "Next time?" For a moment, she was tempted to pull away. But then her body settled in against his and encouraged her brain to accept him so close to her, as well.

"Would that be so hard, do you think?" he asked. "Being together again?"

He was practically daring her to refute him. But of course she couldn't. Being around him was making her feel alive again. Making her feel confident. She shook her head.

Just as she tried to come up with the right words to explain herself, his lips found hers.

And like the night before, his touch made her feel all languid and special. When their kisses deepened, she cuddled closer, enjoying the feel of her breasts against his chest. Cal Riddell was hard and strong everywhere she wasn't. And the contrasts between their bodies was so appealing, she ached to explore them further.

With a groan, Cal's hands found her hips, then one reached up and cupped her breast, his thumb grazing the peak.

She moaned in response, lifted her jaw so he could kiss her neck. And while he was doing that, she gave in to temptation and slid her hand down his hip, along the hard planes of his thigh.

And then, too soon, he pulled away.

"We've got to stop," he said, his voice hoarse. "This kitchen isn't the place for what I want to do."

She knew her eyes were wide as they met his.

"We should go out again—just the two of us—soon."

There was only one answer. "Yes."

"You'll find a babysitter? So we can be alone?"

"I'll try," she said, sounding breathless. "If I find one, I'll let you know."

Tension she didn't even know he had seemed to float from his body. "Thank you."

When they both couldn't seem to stop staring at each other, she coughed. "You know what? I think I'll wash these dishes."

"And I…I'm gonna go check on Ginny and Hank." He turned away and exited before she had a chance to reply.

As Susan stuck her hands in the warm, sudsy water, she realized she could hardly wait to see him again.

Chapter Fifteen

"Susan, are you ever going to sit and talk with me again? Or were those sweet smiles you gave me the first day I was here all for show?"

Susan turned around, and met the piercing blue eyes of Calvin Riddell Sr. He was sitting at a card table behind her, alone for a change. When she raised her brows at his question, he had the gall to widen his eyes in an expression of pure innocence. "Mr. Riddell, what do you mean by that?"

"I mean, you sashay around this place chatting with everyone and anyone…except me. I don't know why."

She hid a smile. She didn't think for a minute that he'd been lonesome for her company. In the space of only a few weeks, Mr. Riddell had become a rather popular man around the retirement home. At first, she'd thought it was because of his last name.

But as the days passed, she was learning that he was a favorite among all the residents because of his personality. People were drawn to him like flies to honey. He had a no-nonsense appeal to him that couldn't be ignored.

Kind of like his son.

"Well? Are you going to answer me, little lady?" he prodded.

Who else would call her that? "Don't call me little lady," she retorted, just to get a rise out of him.

As she'd hoped, he scowled. "Gotta call you something."

"Susan? Ms. Young?"

"I haven't called a pretty lady by her last name in years. I'm too old for that. Now tell me what you know."

"About what?" she sassed. Even she was coming to find out that he was not a man who responded well to sweetness.

"Anything." His lips twitched. "Tell me some gossip. What's the story with all the nurses? Who drives everyone crazy?"

"I don't gossip about people here."

"You should. Or at least, you could make some up. You in the mood to lie to me for a little while?"

"I am. Well, I am until Mrs. Ventura comes in. We have a date to play cards."

"That Rosa." His eyes flashed. "She's a tough cookie."

"She is." As she moved to sit across from him, she looked him over more carefully. "So, truth now. How are you feeling?"

Grayish-blue eyes dimmed a bit. "Truth? Fair to middlin'. I've got less energy than a newborn calf."

"That's to be expected, yes?"

"Probably." He grunted. "But knowin' I'm not supposed to be a hundred percent doesn't make things any easier to take, you know?"

"I know." Eager to see some spark back in his eyes, she asked, "You're not still giving the physical therapists a hard time, are you?"

His lips twitched before he adopted his trademark scowl. "What have you been hearing?"

"I've been hearing that your mouth could use a bar of soap."

"Me?"

"You. I've also heard that you could teach sailors on leave a thing or two." Leaning forward, she whispered, "Not everyone wants to be cussed at, Mr. Riddell."

"Not everyone wants to be poked and prodded, either." Steepling his hands in front of him, he said, "Enough of this. I didn't ask you over here to talk about me."

"What do you want to talk about?"

"My son."

"Cal?"

"Of course Cal. It's not like you know my other boys." He raised an eyebrow. "Or do you?"

"Of course I don't."

"Then tell me what's going on with you and Junior."

What had been happening between the two of them was confusing. And special. "There's not much to tell you. I hardly know Cal...."

"Now I think you're lying again. I think there might be."

"And why is that?"

He winked. "'Cause one of those physical therapists who's been torturing me managed to sneak in a few words about you and Junior the other day."

"And what did she say?"

"She said that you and my middle son went on a date the other night."

"We went walking in town," she clarified.

"That counts." He waggled his brows. "Rumor has it that the two of you looked pretty chummy. That you were sparkin' under the twinkly lights of the town square."

In spite of the fact that she was twenty-five years old, she felt her cheeks heat. "Chummy isn't much of a descriptor."

"It's better than your descriptions. My Cal, he's a good man."

"Are you trying to shoo me away? Or just the opposite?"

"If it was the opposite, it would mean that I approved of you."

The wish that slammed into her scared her half to death. "Do you?"

"Do you need me to?"

"Truth?"

"Of course."

She felt as though they were participating in the verbal equivalent of a chess game. With a sinking feeling, she told the truth. "Yes," she whispered. Then waited.

Laugh lines appeared at the corners of his eyes. "If Junior had to pick a woman to start seeing, and he really thought he needed a woman who was real sassy, and who already had a son, and who actually liked hanging out with old farts all day long…then I guess I'd say you'd do."

"We're not serious, you know."

To her surprise, Calvin chuckled. "Of course y'all are. Cal doesn't do anything *not* serious. Don't you know that by now? What's more, I'm getting the feeling that you don't, either."

"I haven't had any other choice but to take things seriously."

"Nothing wrong with responsibility, Susan. Sometimes I think there's some people who naturally lean toward being stressed out and carry the weight of the world on their shoulders."

"Is that how you were?"

"Nah. I tried to be a rodeo star, but I never had the seat for it. For some reason, I got lucky with my oil find."

She couldn't help but smile at that. "Some would call your oil find a pretty big deal."

"Oh, it was that. But becoming rich at thirty-seven was a difficult thing, let me tell you."

"Rumor has it that you didn't do bad with your find. Gossips have told me you invested it wisely. Doubled your worth."

He scowled. "You sure know a lot for a woman who hates to gossip."

"I didn't say I didn't know how to gossip. I just didn't want to gossip with you."

With an exaggerated wince, Mr. Riddell pressed his hands to his chest. "You're wounding me."

She laughed. "Hopefully not so much. I do like hearing about your successes, though."

Turning wistful, he murmured, "I had a wife and three boys. All of us had a heap of dreams that could suddenly be fulfilled. If that don't humble a person, I don't know what does."

She was about to speak again—about nothing important, she supposed—when a churlish cough erupted behind her. "Ms. Young. Mr. Riddell needs to return to his room. It's time to check his vitals."

"You almost make that sound dirty, Yvonne."

A put-upon, resigned look entered the nurse's aide's eyes. "Mr. Riddell, are you ever going to behave?"

"I hope not," he murmured. "Come on, then." As he started walking, he gave Susan a little wave. "I'll be seeing you. Tell that boy to take you to the ranch."

"We went on Sunday."

"Have fun?"

"Yes, sir."

"Mr. Riddell, I'm waiting."

"Yvonne?" Susan called out.

The aide stilled. "Yes?"

"Please remember to speak to our guests with a bit more care."

A new awareness flickered in the aide's light gold eyes. "I will, Ms. Young."

As they continued, Susan heard Calvin chuckle. "Now, Yvonne, if you'd only smile more, the world would be your oyster."

"Yes, sir."

Susan stood for a moment, watching them walk off together. She felt better about the aide's demeanor when she noticed the woman observe Mr. Riddell's ease of movement and color. Even to Susan's eye, it was obvious that she was concerned about his welfare.

She was about to return to her office, when Rosa Ventura slowly rolled forward in her wheelchair. "Susan, I'm so sorry to keep you waiting. I had a phone call I had to take."

"It's all right. I was visiting with Mr. Riddell until Yvonne came and took him away."

Rosa laughed. "Poor Calvin. That Yvonne is as thorny as they come."

"I'm beginning to realize that," Susan said.

"He's okay, Susan. Don't worry." With a wink, she added, "Actually, Calvin and I have been talking quite a bit lately."

"Is that the reason for your improved spirits?"

"Maybe," she said coyly. "It's nice to have something to look forward to. For a while there, all I could seem to do was think about things in my past. That will getcha every time."

Rosa's words hit her hard. She was exactly right. Susan felt as if her mood, too, had improved when she and Hank had started seeing Cal. "Mrs. Ventura, are you ready for cards?"

"I am. Are you ready to lose?"

Chapter Sixteen

Jarred looked entirely too relaxed and smug beside Cal as they drove over to the north barn at daybreak.

"I've got to tell you, Junior, going to Cancún was a great idea. I told Serena that we ought to go there on our honeymoon, too."

Irritated with his brother's exuberance, Cal pushed the gas with a little too much gumption. The old Chevy retaliated by groaning and jumping over a rut.

Jarred grabbed his armrest. "Junior, what the heck? Take it easy now."

"Sorry." Trying to calm his voice, Cal said, "Honeymoon?"

"Yeah, that's what I said." His brother's perpetually amused expression turned serious. "I asked her to marry me. She said yes."

"Congratulations." Cal frowned as he heard his voice. It sounded choked, as if he could barely force the words out.

"You okay with that?"

"Why would you even ask? Serena's a wonderful woman."

"I know. But you don't seem all that happy about my news."

"I am," Cal replied. "Besides, it doesn't matter all that

much whether I am or not. You're the one talking marriage. Not me." Of course, he'd been thinking about it.

"But you're affected." Jarred frowned. "I thought you liked Seri."

"I do. She's great. Of course she's great."

"You still haven't answered my question."

"I'm fine with that. Of course I'm fine."

"Junior, it may just be me being stupid, but I have a sneaking suspicion that you are being too agreeable."

"You're right. You are being stupid." Mentally, Cal called himself ten times the fool. His brother needed his support, not his whining. "Hell, Jarred, we all knew you and Serena were friends for years. The two of you make a great couple."

Jarred's shoulders relaxed. "I thought so, too. I think we make a real good one. She makes me happy. She makes me happy in a way that I hadn't dreamed possible. In Mexico, we walked on the beach, and even went to some of those tourist spots." His eyes grew wider. "Shoot, we did all kinds of stuff I never thought I'd ever do." He shook his head in wonder. "We went parasailing."

"You hate all that tourist stuff."

"I do…but it was fun, seeing things through her eyes."

"You deserve her."

"Thanks." Leaning forward, he turned businesslike. "So, how is everything? I know I've left you in the lurch, what with Dad in rehab, Trent in the hospital and Ginny being as six as ever. What do you need me to take care of?"

What didn't he need help with? "How much time do you have? An hour to spare?"

His brother bristled. "Don't talk to me like that. You know I've done my part for years."

Cal knew that. Of course, he'd felt as if he'd been doing

his part and then some for just about that long. "Sorry. Dad being at the Lodge has really set me off."

"Because of his heart? I thought the doctors said he was going to be okay." Jarred's voice deepened, illustrating how worried he was.

"He is. It's different now, you know? It's like I finally realized that Dad isn't invincible."

"I had that same realization a few months ago. It sucks, don't it?"

"Yeah." What he didn't say—what was really bothering him—was that everything was changing, sometimes too fast. And he, the guy who liked to keep everything in control, was having a difficult time keeping up with it all.

"Here's what we're going to do. I'm going to take over things for a few days. You give yourself a break."

"And do what? Take off to Cancún?"

"If you want. Or, at the very least, you could get out of here for an afternoon or night. Do something fun."

Fun? "I forgot what that's like."

"That's your problem, Junior," Jarred said with an exaggerated shake of his head. "If you have to be reminded about what fun is, then you definitely need to get out more often."

Cal nodded, but his head was spinning. Because there was only one person he wanted to be with and that was Susan. "Have I told you that I'm glad you're back?"

Jarred flashed his trademark smile. "Now you have. Thanks for that. For the record, I'm glad to be home."

SUSAN HADN'T SEEN BETSY too much over the past few days. Even though they'd patched things up, she wasn't sure if they were back on solid ground again.

She'd been busy with work, though, and so hadn't worried about it too much. It was only late at night, when Hank was asleep and her body was exhausted but her mind wide awake, that Susan yearned for their girl talks. Watching *Law & Order* didn't give her the same degree of satisfaction.

Two nights ago, she'd called Betsy, just to see if she wanted to stop by, but her friend hadn't been home. She'd decided not to leave a message.

But now, as she saw Betsy's distinctive red hair through the glass door, Susan couldn't have been happier.

"Hey. Want a glass of wine?"

"Not tonight. I'm just sipping tea."

"Are you sick?"

Betsy sighed. "Maybe. I don't know." Looking almost disgruntled, she whispered, "Susan, I think I might be lovesick, if you want to know the truth."

Betsy looked so distraught, it was comical. But Susan did her best to fight off a smile. "How's Gene?"

"Great. Last night we went out for ice cream. Two nights ago, we had dinner with his sister and her husband."

Susan couldn't resist teasing her. "Uh-oh. If you're meeting relatives, things might be getting serious."

"Oh, they are." She shook her head in wonder. "He kisses like a dream, too. Who would have thought?"

Susan couldn't help it, she sighed. Whenever she let herself, her mind drifted back to Cal and the kisses they'd shared on their walk. Those kisses had been dreamlike, too.

As if reading her mind, Betsy said, "Actually, I came over to talk about you, not me. How are things going with you and Cal Riddell?"

"Pretty good. We went out to the ranch the other day. And I've been seeing him every now and then at the Lodge."

"And?"

"And we have a date scheduled for Saturday night."

"There you go. Maybe y'all are heading toward love, too."

"I'm not sure about that. Not too long ago, I could hardly stand to be in the same building as him."

Betsy's eyes crinkled over the rim of the mug she was sipping. "But then, things changed...."

"Perhaps."

"Well, like I said before, y'all sure looked cozy at Bob's. There's something right between you two."

"We do have an attraction, I can't deny that."

"All relationships start there, don't you think?"

"Maybe. I'm not sure."

"Susan, what's wrong? If Cal Riddell liked me, I wouldn't let him out of my sight! Honey, if you had him, you could be set for life."

She didn't like the direction the conversation was taking. And she liked even less the sly, niggling thought in the back of her mind that agreed with Betsy.

If, for some crazy reason, she and Cal did go heading down the aisle, she *would* be set for life. And even more important, Hank would be.

But at what cost?

"I don't want to think about Cal that way." Because, well, sometimes she did.

"Susan—"

"No, when you talk about all his money, it makes me feel dirty, like I'm using him."

"We know you're not. But you'd be naive not to consider how his money could change your life. You have a boy to support."

"That doesn't matter to me."

Betsy looked her over as she stood up. "You know, once upon a time—oh, about three weeks ago—I would have called you crazy. Now, though, I'm beginning to think you've been right all along. I like Gene. I like going to his family's house and having dinner. And watching football next to him on the couch." She blinked. "None of that costs much at all. I'm suddenly deciding it's not a secure future I should be thinking about, it's a happy today."

Susan smiled weakly. Betsy was right. Having good days did count for a lot.

Maybe even more than worrying about past mistakes or problematic futures.

"I'm glad you came over, Betsy. I really am."

"I am, too. Take care now."

When she was alone again, Susan couldn't help but let her mind wander to the possibilities of taking the security that a rich man offered.

Surely she'd like Cal even if he didn't have the ranch and the money and the connections, right?

Surely those attributes didn't even factor into her change of heart with him…did they?

Chapter Seventeen

"Susan, it's so good to hear your voice."

"Mr. Norton, I have to say I'm pretty surprised to hear from you," Susan replied, juggling her cell phone while walking through Electra Elementary's open house.

He chuckled. "I know I'm calling out of the blue, but I wondered if you could spare me a few minutes of your time."

Well, this wasn't a good time. Ever since she'd gotten home from work, Hank had been talking about the open house. She didn't want to neglect him.

But for the life of her, she didn't want to push off this call, either. If she didn't talk to Mr. Norton tonight, she'd have to wait until tomorrow.

And that would drive her crazy. "Of course, if you could hold on just one sec?"

"Sure. Take your time."

Putting her hand over the receiver, she walked over to Hank, who was standing in front of a line of artwork. "Hank, I need to take this call."

He shot her a look full of disappointment. "But we've got to go in my room so you can meet my teacher."

"As soon as I'm off the phone, I'll do that. Now, you can wait right here, or you can go in the room without me."

"I'll go in," he said.

"I'll hurry. I promise." She smiled, but he'd already turned his back on her and gone in the room. Susan felt terrible, but she still brought the phone back up to her ear. "Mr. Norton, I'm sorry. I'm at a school meeting."

"Sure you can take my call?"

"I'm sure."

"Well, it's like this. We've had some restructuring here and I'm now the director."

"Oh, my. Congratulations!"

"I thought you might be happy to hear about that," he replied, a smile in his voice. "It was pretty evident that there hasn't been a lot of love lost between you and Ms. Wynn." He cleared his throat. "Susan, I'm calling to see if you would be interested in having my old job."

"As assistant director?" As other parents walked by, some looking at her curiously, her heart started beating double time.

"Exactly."

"Wow, this is quite a surprise."

He chuckled. "I thought it might be. Listen, it's just as well you're busy now, because I don't want you to do anything but think about this for a day or two. But please know that you're our first choice, and the board has told me that I can offer you a very competitive salary."

When he told her the amount, she closed her eyes. It was a full twenty thousand more than she'd been making when she left. And it was a whole lot more than what she was making in Electra.

"Oh, my gosh," she said, practically choking.

"I thought that might catch your attention," he said. "Well, I'll let you get back to your meeting. But think about it and give us a call soon. Okay?"

"Yes, sir. Thank you."

After clicking off, she raced in to see Hank.

He was standing next to his desk, staring at the doorway. His face lit up when she walked to his side. "I'm all done, honey. And I'm sorry about that. Now, show me all around. Is this your desk?"

He nodded. "Uh-huh. And this is Miss Shay."

Susan shook the young teacher's hand. "It's a pleasure to meet you."

"Hank's doing great," Miss Shay said. "I'm glad he's in my classroom."

Beside her, Hank beamed.

After they exchanged a few more pleasantries, Hank grabbed her hand and showed her their class turtle, their cubbies, his reading book and their calendar by the door.

Next, he took her toward the art room. Walking down the hall, Susan smiled. "You really like your school, don't you?"

"Uh-huh. Well, I mean, I'm starting to."

She was about to ask him some questions, when they came upon Cal and Ginny. Hank came to an abrupt stop and grinned. "Hey, Mr. Riddell. Hey, Ginny."

After a brief nod in her direction, Cal leaned toward Hank. "You showing your mother your classroom, Hank?"

"Uh-huh. Now we're going to look at the art room."

"We just came from there," Ginny said importantly.

"Hank, you going to come over for another riding lesson soon?"

A look of pure wonder filled his face. "Yeah. I mean, yessir."

Right then and there, Cal Riddell chuckled. "Hank, you speak to me like that, I'm going to think you're Texan!"

"I'm getting to be one," Hank said with a little lift of his chin.

And that made Susan more confused than ever.

Patting the boy's shoulder, Cal said, "I'll ask your mother to bring you over soon."

With a brief salute her way, Cal left, Ginny skipping down the hall by his side.

"Did you hear that?" Hank asked. "Did you hear Mr. Riddell say I can come over soon? And that I almost sounded Texan?"

"I did," Susan said with a smile.

Of course, she'd also heard Cal laugh. And that had to be one of the sweetest sounds ever.

AS THE OPENING CREDITS appeared on the large screen in the middle of the field, Cal glanced her way. "Funny how things worked out, huh?"

"It's hard to believe, that's what it is." When Cal had called her on Friday night, he'd suggested a date to the drive-in with the kids.

Then, earlier today, he'd called again. This time to ask if Hank could come over to watch videos with Ginny and Gwen—and to see the new kittens in the barn—while the two of them went out.

It had taken less than two seconds for Hank to decide he'd much rather do that than sit in a truck with his mom all evening.

And now here they were. Alone in the dark.

"Did you know that this is what I've been thinking about all day?" Cal whispered just inches from her lips. "Is this what you had in mind when you agreed to go to the drive-in?"

"Actually, no..."

"No?" he drawled. As his lips brushed her jaw, his tongue flicked at a spot under her ear. "What were you thinking about?"

Um...did it really matter?

No. It didn't matter at all as one of his hands curved around her rib cage. As the other cupped the back of her head. As his lips claimed hers.

She shifted and cuddled closer, and kissed him back. And held on...because it was like lightning had struck. There was no other way to describe it. Heat enveloped them. Heat and attraction and...want. With a moan, she moved even closer. Tilted her head so he could deepen the kiss. Though, really...it had never been a tentative thing at all.

No, from the first moment he'd touched her, there had been a current between them. Fast and hot. His tongue swiped against her teeth, murmured something, then he gently bit her bottom lip.

She melted. Just like that.

It was almost hard to breathe.

Moments later, panting, he leaned his head against the back of his seat, but she could tell that he was as overcome as she was. His hands were still on her.

"Susan, I'm old enough to be more patient, but for the life of me, all I want to do right now is kiss you. Hold you close. Why do you think that is?"

"I don't know. I've been feeling the same way, too."

That declaration spurred another embrace. Oh, but things were getting out of hand fast and furiously.

When Cal came up for air, his breathing was ragged. "Do you want to stop? Are we going too fast?"

She knew what he was saying. Ever the gentleman, he was giving her options. Giving her space. If all she wanted to do that evening was watch a movie, eat popcorn and kiss, that was all that was going to happen.

But oh, that was not what she wanted at all. "I don't want to stop."

"Yeah?"

She almost laughed at the relief she heard in his tone. She couldn't blame him; she felt relief, too. There was something to be said for knowing you were about to have sex.

Especially when it had been a really long time. *Years.*

Reaching out, she curved a hand around his neck. Enjoyed the way his skin felt…so different from her own. "I'm not going to pretend I don't want you, Cal. I do. There's something about you that I can't resist."

"I feel the same way. I think you're gorgeous. At first, I thought that was the problem."

"Problem?"

"The problem with me, not you, of course. I didn't want to feel like I do, if you want to know the truth. I didn't want to think about you so much. I didn't want to feel out of control. Everything inside me was screaming for order."

"And peace," she murmured, completely agreeing.

"For too long, I've kept myself hard at work, only thinking about what needed to be done, not what I wanted. But damn it to hell, Susan. I want you like nothing else I've known."

Her whole body reacted. Her breath hitched, her body went on alert. Waiting for him to touch her. Just waiting. Turning to him, she reached for his chest. Felt how solid it was under her hands. Felt the muscles, the smooth skin under the starched cotton. "Kiss me again?"

He complied. Once again, there was nothing tentative. His lips were firm, demanding. Teeth clashed against each other as they both fought the urge to pin down their desires. His hands clenched her waist, pulling her toward him. One palm covered her breast, his thumb tracing over the tip.

She responded by pushing against him and looping one thigh over his. Aching to be on top.

Neatly, he reversed their positions and he had her lying

on the bench seat of his truck, her legs open under his, his jeans and her skirt the only barrier. Hardly aware of doing it, Susan lifted the ends of her white frothy peasant blouse and pulled it over her head. Seconds later, she'd unhooked her bra and tossed it on the floor.

"Damn," he said, then leaned down again, warming her skin with his cotton-covered chest. With his hands. Then finally, with his lips and tongue. His cheek was slightly rough, as if he'd shaved that afternoon, but not very well. Or maybe it was just that her skin was so sensitized to his own that every nuance, every movement between them was exaggerated. More pronounced.

She smelled his fresh, clean scent. Tasted the faint taste of mint, the slightest hint of coffee…

His fingers were slightly callused, abrading her skin, making her melt. She nipped at his neck, heard an answering moan of appreciation, then pretty much forgot everything except how delicious it was to feel his weight on her, how attentive he was, how perfect he was…as his lips claimed hers again.

Minutes passed, or maybe it was an hour.

The seat creaked underneath them. Her hands cupped him through his jeans; his hand did the same with her.

Finally, he broke away, panting. "We have to stop," he said. "I can't do this any longer. This is definitely not where I want to make love with you." He pulled away, digging under the seat for his shirt. It had come off just moments after his lips had touched her stomach.

Little by little, reality returned, making Susan realize that they only had the semblance of privacy. Thankful for the dark, for the fogged windows, for the faint glow of the movie still playing, Susan sat up as well and fumbled for her bra. Finally she found it. With a sigh, she did her best to untangle the white lace, and then noticed him staring at her. She smiled. She, too, could have looked at him all night.

"You're beautiful," he said. "I've rarely seen something that takes my breath away like you do."

She merely smiled and fastened the clip behind her, then hastily slipped her shirt back on.

"We should probably at least be heading back to the ranch. I mean, the kids are there." He paused. "But maybe we don't need to go inside to see the kids right away." A crooked smile turned her way. "What do you say, Susan? Want to go parking?"

She was twenty-five years old. She had a son and a demanding job. At the moment, she wanted nothing more than to go parking with Cal Riddell. "Of course."

"Thank God. Buckle up, honey."

FEELING SUSPICIOUSLY like a teenage boy about to lose his virginity, Cal drove the truck back to the ranch, keeping one hand securely on Susan's knee.

He decided he truly deserved a medal for keeping his hand there. All night long, that flirty skirt of hers had played with his insides, turning his stomach into knots, encouraging his fingers to drift a little higher...to caress her thighs.

Now her knees were slightly apart, and her hip was resting against his. It didn't help things that just a little while ago, he'd had his hands a whole lot higher than her knee, and that she'd given him nothing but encouragement along the way.

Desperate for relief, he turned the air conditioner on high and tilted the vent his way. When the cold air blasted his face, he hoped it would cool the rest of him off. Warily, he looked Susan's way.

Oh, she'd noticed what he was doing, all right. She

smiled a little helplessly. "Is it always so warm at night in September?"

"Not always." He swallowed. No, he hadn't been this hot in weeks. Shoot, months, most likely.

She shifted uncomfortably. "No, I imagine not."

They were now less than five minutes from the ranch's entrance. Maybe it was the cold air, maybe it was the idea that they were so close to getting what they wanted. And still so far from how he'd imagined making love to her that he pried his palm from her knee and gave her fingers a squeeze. "Anyone looking at us from a distance would think we're a couple of teenagers."

"Until they saw us up close."

"And then they'd be shocked, hmm?" He braked as he made the turn onto his land. He drove slowly as he waited for her to come to her senses. For her to tell him that there was no way in hell she was going to let them get naked on the bench seat of his Chevy.

But she said nothing, only continued to look a little bemused, whether from what they were doing or where he was taking her, he didn't know.

It was obviously up to him to return them to reason. "Sue, there's a thicket in our north pasture. I thought we could park there. No one will bother us. Shoot, no one will even be able to see the truck, the trees and brush are so thick. If…that's what you want."

"Do you?"

"I'm driving you there, aren't I?"

When she blinked in surprise, he tempered his voice. Remembering that women needed to hear the words. "It's still what I want."

"It's still what I want, too," she said softly.

In no time, he'd parked the truck and shut the lights.

The moon wasn't out, and it was dark in the cab. As his eyes adjusted, he could barely make out her silhouette.

There was only one thing to do. He pulled her into his arms and started kissing her, quietly doing his best to bring her back to the point where they'd stopped earlier.

To the point that had brought them out here.

Susan responded enthusiastically. Her mouth was open, her tongue probing into his mouth. Her hands were pulling at his shirt.

He easily unbuttoned the three top buttons and pulled it over his head. To his pleasure, she slipped out of that top and bra again, then slid her hands up his bare chest.

Scant moments later, his jeans were off and her panties were down, and protection was in his hand.

He was embarrassed. Surely she'd expected a little more grace? More patience? "I'm sorry. Can't wait, Sue." Before he lost his mind, he prepared himself for her. And then suddenly he was home. Or what it felt like, anyway.

Her legs were wrapped around him, her breath was coming in short bursts, her hands were on his ass. Only a few hard thrusts brought them both to fulfillment.

Slowly, reality settled back in. Sweat coated his shoulders, his back. In the dim light, Susan was staring up at him, something akin to wonder in her eyes.

"Was I too rough?" he murmured. "It's been a long time for me. Jeez, I promise I usually have a bit more finesse."

"Finesse in your truck?" She laughed. "Oh, the things you worry about, Cal."

She was joking. She wasn't disappointed. She didn't have regrets. "Maybe next time we could spread out a bit?"

She sighed, as if he was asking too much of her. "Just tell me when and where, Cal Riddell. And I'll be there."

"Is tomorrow too soon?"

"Not at all," she whispered before she leaned up and

touched her lips to his. "As a matter of fact, tomorrow's way too late."

"Guess you don't mind the truck?" he murmured against her lips, rubbed his hands along her back, enjoyed the way her cool, soft skin felt against his fingers.

"Nope."

"So then, maybe, we could—"

"Stop talking, Cal, and kiss me."

Cal Riddell did the only thing he could do. He easily complied with her wishes. It wasn't hard to do.

Chapter Eighteen

"How much longer is Daddy going to be staying at the care center?" Ginny asked as Cal pulled in to a parking space at the front of the home two days later.

Jarred, who was sitting in the passenger seat next to Cal, looked over his shoulder and answered, "I'm not rightly sure, sugar. A lot depends on how he's feeling."

"Is he feeling better?"

"I think so," Cal said. Actually, most of the time when he'd visited, he had a feeling his father was having the time of his life at the retirement home. He'd only seen his dad sit alone in his room a handful of times. Actually, most times, Cal had a heck of a time trying to figure out where his father was. Feeling stronger, he was now walking out by the pond, playing poker with the other men, and had even taken to playing gin with Rosa Ventura on a regular basis.

When Cal came to visit, they focused on people his dad had met, or the other old guys. Or the family. Rarely did he ask about the day-to-day operation of the ranch anymore.

Instead, he talked of it in general terms…almost as if his ranching days were in his past.

Yet there was still Ginny to consider. She needed him, too.

"But Daddy will come home soon?" she asked. "You really think so?"

"I do." Glancing in the rearview mirror, Cal saw that Ginny's expression was full of worry. While Cal could imagine his father enjoying things other than the ranch, poor Ginny just missed her father. "He will," he promised.

Lightening his tone, Cal looked over at his brother, who was texting on his cell. "Jarred, you were here yesterday. Did any of the nurses tell you anything? I wonder if I should contact Dr. Williams. You know, to get a full report."

"Whatever you think," Jarred replied as he slipped his cell phone into his back pocket. "Though, I have to admit that I haven't asked about his EDD lately."

Cal shook his head. His brother loved acronyms, and it took practically a psychic to figure them out. "EDD?"

"Estimated Date of Departure. What else?"

"Oh, brother." Because a child was present, Cal refrained from telling Jarred that he was acting like an SOB. "Virginia, we'll ask Susan if she knows anything about when Dad's coming home. If anyone knows what's going on around there, she will."

As Jarred folded his seat forward so Ginny could climb out of the back, he had the gall to wink at their little sister. "Oh, yes. Let's ask Susan all about Dad's EDD when we see her. Because I'm sure there's no other reason why Junior would want to see Susan."

With a click of a button, Cal locked the doors, then tried to glare at Jarred the best he could without Ginny noticing. "Watch it," he warned under his breath.

Ginny grabbed Jarred's hand and started skipping along beside him. "I like Susan."

"I can't wait to meet this lady myself," Jarred said. "She seems to be all our usually solemn brother can talk about.

In fact, I have a feeling we're going to cross paths with her first thing. She might even be just around the corner, waiting to greet us."

"Enough," Cal muttered.

Jarred chuckled. "Settle down. I'm just joshing ya. You're due, anyway. We both know I got lots of grief from you about Serena."

But Serena was Jarred's fiancée. They were serious. Cal swallowed. Was that the direction he was headed with Susan? Matrimony?

When they entered through the automatic doors, even the blessed coolness of the air conditioner couldn't save Cal's cheeks from heating up...or stop his heartbeat from accelerating when he spied Susan.

"Hi," she said with a smile. "I was hoping I'd get a chance to see you when you came in."

Today, Susan had on a black skirt that did nice things to her hips and a bright pink knit shirt cut in a low V across the front. Lace along the edge almost made it look modest, but even that swath of lace couldn't disguise the inch or so of cleavage that was visible to everyone who dared to look.

And who wouldn't look? As always, she was gorgeous. And that pink top seemed to make her auburn hair look even more striking than usual.

Beside him, his brother's smile turned into a full-fledged grin. "Hi," he said. "I'm Jarred. And I know you already know Ginny."

Susan smiled at Ginny. "I sure do. She and my son, Hank, are becoming good friends." Holding out a hand, she said, "I'm Susan Young. It's a pleasure to meet you, too." When Cal took Ginny over to say hello to Paula, Susan stepped closer to Jarred.

He shook her hand. "Same. So, I hear you're new to Electra?"

"I am. Hank and I just moved here a few months ago."

"Electra's a small town. I'm surprised we haven't crossed paths before."

"I am, too." She shrugged. "But I've been working a lot. I don't have much spare time."

"I know what that's like. I heard you've been out to our place?"

"I have. Cal took me around." Susan smiled Cal's way. "It's really beautiful. You're lucky to have such a pretty place to call home."

"Where is home for you?"

"Ohio. The Cincinnati area."

"Long way to move for a job," Jarred commented. Almost easy sounding. *Almost,* but not quite.

"It was."

"But you've settled in?"

"I'm trying to. I'm one of the directors here. I'm in charge of human resources."

"But I suppose you're lookin' to put down roots and such."

"I hope so, I mean we will, if we end up staying."

Jarred paused. "*If* you end up staying? But I thought you and Cal were getting close."

"Well, we are kind of close, but I can't stay here just for him," she replied. "I mean, when or if we break up, I'll have nothing."

The moment her words left her mouth, Susan wished she could take them back. Then she could clarify her thinking. Explain how she needed security in her life, one way or another. That Hank needed at least that from her.

But she didn't owe Cal's brother more of an explanation. Especially when Jarred was glaring at her the way he was, as if she had said she liked torturing small animals.

Whenever they'd discussed the other Riddell brothers,

all Betsy had ever mentioned was Jarred's fabulous charm. She'd even told Susan a story about how Jarred had participated in the town's charity event...even going so far as to auction himself off to the winning lady.

In Susan's mind, that had to have taken a lot of confidence and swagger. But little of that seemed to be in evidence today.

So far, Susan thought his questions were just a little too pointed for comfort.

"So, do you have any idea what you'll do if you leave here? If—or when—things with Cal don't work out?"

"Yes. Just the other day I got a call from my old job in Cincinnati. They offered me a promotion if I'd come back."

Jarred narrowed his eyes. "You'd do that? Just take off?"

"Maybe. I've got bills to pay." Darting a look Cal's way, she added, "I imagine I'll have to go if I don't have a good reason to stay."

"Because you need the job."

That wasn't it at all. What she wanted was a commitment from Cal one day. But that thought was too special and too private to say out loud to Cal's brother. So she retorted with a quip. "Definitely. Not everyone has your kind of money, Jarred," she added with a smile.

Then, of course, she wished she'd never said that at all. "Um, would y'all like me to walk you down to your father's wing?"

"That's not necessary. We've got it. I promise, we don't need a thing more from you."

"JARRED, WHAT IS GOING ON?" Cal asked as he approached, just in time to hear his brother speak way too rudely to Susan.

"Nothing," Jarred said as he motioned Cal forward.

"Hold on, now. Susan, what's wrong?" Cal asked.

"Excuse me," she said. "I need to make a call."

Warily, Cal watched her walk away, then turned on his brother. "What did you do?"

"I've been getting to the truth," Jarred said as they began to slowly walk down the hall. "Susan told me that she's been considering a job back in Ohio."

"No, she's not."

"I promise you, she is," Jarred said grimly. "Obviously, she's been keeping secrets from you."

"I bet she was going to tell me about that job," Cal said. But even to his ears, his words sounded forced.

"Look. The fact of the matter is that Susan's on the hunt for money. And if she can't get it from you, she's going to get it from somewhere else."

Cal was stunned to silence.

Were things that messed up between them? Was she really looking to leave? Every part of him wanted to ask her about that. To get her to clarify things. But now wasn't the time because Jarred pushed his way into their father's room, Ginny started carrying on...and from inside, his father called out his name.

Feeling his cheeks heat again, he nodded, then followed his family inside. And told himself he'd try to figure out what was going on with his brother sooner than later.

WHEN THE TRIO OF RIDDELLS were out of sight, Susan practically ran to her office and shut the door. She was too stunned and bewildered by what had just happened.

Why had she told Jarred all those things?

She was sure he would tell Cal what she'd said and Cal would read it all wrong.

Old hurts and distrust rose to the surface again. Greg had been that way, too. He'd gone from sweet and loving to distant and gone within minutes of finding out about her pregnancy.

She never would have imagined Cal turning away from her, not after what they'd shared.

But maybe—just maybe—he wasn't as genuine as she'd started to imagine he was?

Oh, this confusion hurt.

She forced herself to understand why it hurt so much.

But actually, she knew the reason was simple. She'd fallen in love with him.

Really, how could she have been so foolish?

Almost without her knowing, she'd begun to trust him. To imagine a life with him. Obviously, she should have gotten her head around the idea that whatever had been happening between them, it hadn't been a mutual thing.

Maybe not a mutual thing at all.

Chapter Nineteen

Cal's father had been oddly reluctant to visit with them. As a matter of fact, as soon as they'd gotten all the pleasantries out of the way, he'd hugged Ginny, asked Jarred about Mexico and Serena and then acted as if he couldn't wait for them to leave.

So much so that Cal had even teased him about it. "Is our visit keeping you from something, Dad?"

"As a matter of fact, yes. There's a social here this afternoon. A couple of the guys and me were going to play a few rounds of Texas Hold'em."

Jarred frowned. "You're blowing us off to play poker?"

"I am. I'm scheduled to leave in four days. So, I'm going to play as much poker as I can." Glaring at all three of them, he barked, "Y'all got a problem with it?"

Jarred blinked. "No, sir."

By his side, even Ginny had held her tongue.

"Well, then," Jarred said. "I guess we'll let you get to it, then."

"I'll stop by tomorrow," Cal promised.

"I'm sure you will. Your girl's here."

Moments later, Jarred glared his way when they were walking back down the hall. "I really think you should reconsider this relationship you've got with Susan."

"I've gathered that."

"Are you going to take my advice?"

"No."

"You should."

"What is that supposed to mean? What, you've got an opinion about Susan after five minutes?"

Jarred pointedly looked at Ginny. "We can talk about it later."

"Oh, we will," Cal promised.

An hour later, after they got back home and Ginny was visiting with Serena, Cal glared at his brother. "Would you care to tell me more about this conversation you had?"

"Not especially."

"Oh, no. You start talking. Back at the Lodge, you couldn't wait to give me dirt on her."

"All I'm going to say is that while I know you like her, she's not the right woman for you."

"First of all, I didn't say we were getting married. We're still trying to figure things out."

"I think she's really trying to figure out how much of an easy target you are. She's thinking about your money and this ranch."

"And you got all that from a five-minute conversation?"

"She reminded me of other girls we know who are out for a sugar daddy."

"Such as?"

"Oh, I don't know." Jarred paused for a moment, then snapped his fingers. "She was kind of acting like Betsy Carpenter, that's who. You know what she's like! She was after Trent, then you last summer."

"Susan's not like her at all."

"She may say that, but you don't really know for sure, do you? It sounded to me like she really was going to leave if she didn't get a better reason to stay." Jarred put a hand on Cal's shoulder. "She's after a ring, Junior. She wants your ring on her finger so she can trap you well and good. You know I'm right about that."

Cal felt stunned. He couldn't believe Jarred thought Susan was using him. "She's not after my money," he said, shaking off his brother's hand.

"Maybe not, but she might be a lot more interested than you think. A lot of girls aren't afraid to go after anyone who can give them a comfortable lifestyle."

"Not Susan."

"All right. Let's take money and security out of the equation. How about that other thing she mentioned? That she might not even be staying? Doesn't that sound a whole lot like Christy and what she did to you? She left you when she didn't think you were good enough for her."

Cal wasn't about to admit it, but he'd been stewing about that some, too. "She's a nice lady, Jarred. And she's got enough on her plate without you spewing nonsense about her."

Quietly, Jarred said, "Cal, I'd trust you with just about anything. I know you're responsible for keeping everything running the last few months. I trust you with it all. But when it comes to women, you've got no sense, and even less experience. You've been so burned by Christy, you've been keeping to yourself for too long. I just hate to see that Susan is going to hurt you the same way." With a sigh, he said, "You just need to let her go, Junior."

"It's not that easy."

Jarred rolled his eyes. "It's only going to get harder. How long have you known her? What? A month? That sure as hell ain't long enough to get to know what someone's really like. I sure hope you didn't go and screw her."

Cal's temper flared. With cool precision, he hauled off and threw his right fist into his older brother's jaw. Jarred stumbled backward. "Hey!"

Cal clenched his sore hand. "Don't say another word, or so help me, I'll hit you again." Cal stood erect, muscles braced, ready to hit his brother again.

But instead of looking as if he was going to fight back, Jarred raised both hands up in defeat. "I won't," he said softly. "I'm sorry. You know I'm only trying to look out for my little brother. I…I was out of line."

"That's probably the smartest thing you've said today," Cal replied before turning and walking away.

"Then let me say something else. If she's all that and a piece of bread…why don't you let things simmer off for a while. Let some time pass. If she's your future wife, there's no hurry. Let her decide if she's willing to stay here and settle in. Or if she's going to take off."

Though Cal had turned his back on his brother, a part of him started thinking that maybe Jarred did have a point.

Maybe he had pushed things a little fast.

His boots led him through the house. A minute later, he let the kitchen door slam behind him. If his mother had been around, she would have yanked him by the ear and told him a thing or two.

As he strode to the barn, his temper cooled.

And that's when he knew if his mother had been alive, he would have deserved every bit of reprimand she could have come up with.

Because, although he was sure Jarred was wrong…there was a little part of him that feared that he wasn't wrong at all.

That, in fact, Jarred was exactly right. Maybe Susan's feelings weren't as genuine as his. Maybe she did just see him as the answer to her problems. Maybe she said she cared for him, but wouldn't mind picking up and leaving him, just for the hope of something better.

Maybe she wasn't the woman he had imagined her to be—and he'd been too much of a fool to see it.

Maybe she was more like Christy than he'd ever guessed.

When he was alone in the barn, he hung his head in shame. Only a fool would fall for the same thing twice.

Before he could chicken out, he plucked his cell phone out of his back pocket and dialed her number.

She answered on the first ring. "Cal?"

"Hey."

"Is everything all right?" Doubt and worry filled her voice.

"It is. My dad's doing better. I think we're going to bring him home in a few days."

"Ah. I see." She paused. "So, is this why you called?"

"No…" He closed his eyes and forced himself to be tough. To remember how badly Christy had hurt him. "I was just thinking that maybe we've been taking things too fast."

"Too fast?" she repeated, her voice faint.

"Yes. I mean, I've been thinking that maybe we need to put some space between us for a while. You know, slow things down. Especially since you're looking for new jobs and all."

"I shouldn't have blurted out that news to your brother. I didn't go looking to go back to Cincinnati."

"But you're not going to turn it down?"

"Not right away. It's a great opportunity. And then I'd get to be back at home."

Back at home. Great opportunity. "What about Hank?" he asked, too chicken to put himself and his needs in the conversation.

"Hank will be sad, but he'll get over it."

"It sounds like you've already made up your mind."

"I haven't, but I'm seriously considering it."

She was going to leave. And because he couldn't just sit around and be left behind again, he gathered his courage and took the bull by the horns. "If it's all the same to you, I think it might be best if we call things off now. You know. Before things get serious."

After a pause, Susan replied, "That's a good idea. I mean, I'd hate for things to get too serious between us. It would be awful if that happened."

When they clicked off, Cal felt like the biggest heel in the world. He'd really hurt her. Badly.

And if that pain in his chest was any indication, he had the most terrible feeling that he had just hurt himself, too.

Damn.

Chapter Twenty

"Mom?" Hank whispered at the side of her bed a full week after everything had exploded with Cal. "Mom?"

A strong sense of panic compelled Susan to open her eyes. She knew that tone of voice. It was the one her son used when he wasn't feeling well. "What's wrong?"

"I'm dizzy. Real dizzy."

Sitting up, she turned on the light to get a better look at him. His skin was pasty white and his pupils were dilated. "Sit down, honey. Let me get dressed." Her heart raced. She knew they needed to get to the hospital.

This was yet another time when she wished she wasn't alone. If she wasn't alone, she could have someone to lean on. Could have someone to look to for help. Shoot, she could even have someone to simply look at her and nod. To say she was doing everything right.

But of course there wasn't anyone like that.

Rushing to the bathroom, she threw on some clothes, ran a brush through her hair and rinsed out her mouth. Next came the frantic gathering of his insulin shots, his glucose monitor, and a quick grab of one of his stuffed toys.

"Hank, do you want your stuffed bear or tiger?" she called out. When a full minute passed, she ran out to where she'd left him on the couch. "Hank? Hank!"

He'd passed out. Frantically, she dialed 911 and talked to the dispatcher as paramedics were summoned.

Even though her mouth was answering all the woman's questions as coherently as possible, her mind kept running away with itself.

Maybe all her worst fears were coming true. What if he was slipping into a coma? Or worse?

"Hang in there, ma'am," the dispatcher said. "The team should be there five minutes, tops."

Oh! This was all her fault! Maybe she should have given him an injection the very second he woke her up. Why did she waste time getting dressed?

"ETA is three minutes, Ms. Young."

"Uh-huh," Susan murmured, kneeling next to her boy. "Hank? Hank, come on now. Let's go."

Thirty seconds passed. Oh, how could three minutes go by so slow?

Then, he opened one eye. "Mommy?"

Tears pricked her eyes just as the emergency medical technicians knocked on her door. "Mrs. Young?"

Flying from Hank's side, she threw open the door. "In here!" she said. "Hank's in here."

As Hank groggily watched the technicians, they began doing all kinds of things with needles.

"Ma'am? You can hang up the phone now," one of the men said. "We've got your son."

Susan stepped to the side as they loaded Hank onto a stretcher and carefully buckled him in.

Though it killed her to do so, she told them she'd follow in her car. As much as she would rather stay with Hank, she would need her own vehicle later.

She put on a brave face and kissed Hank as they put him in the ambulance, then she locked the door and raced to her car.

She passed every speed limit and counted the minutes until she reached the hospital. After parking the car, she strode through the emergency-room doors and identified herself.

The pretty blonde admissions nurse directed her to a chair. "Ms. Young, they just took your son into an examining room. The doctor's with him now. Please take a moment and help me get him registered."

Though it was the last thing she wanted to do, Susan bit her lip and concentrated on what the nurse was asking of her. Wearily, she gave her address and insurance information, and then obediently went to the chair the woman told her to sit in.

Ten minutes later, she was brought back to Hank.

Even at first glance, she knew her son was doing better. He was sitting on an examining table, his bare feet banging against the metal bars underneath. His eyes were alert and some of his color had returned. An IV was attached to his hand and a new Band-Aid covered the inside of his elbow. Standing next to him was the doctor on duty, a man about her age who was already losing his hair.

"Mom!" Hank called out when he noticed her in the doorway. "Hi."

With a look in the doctor's direction, she slowly walked in and rumpled her son's hair. "You look so much better."

"I feel better."

Every muscle in her body seemed to sag with relief. Turning to the doctor, she held out a hand. "Hi. I'm Susan Young, Hank's mom."

"Leo Kent," he said crisply, betraying a Northern accent that seemed strangely out of place in the Texas hospital. "I was just telling your boy here that we're going to give him some fluids for a while."

"How is he, really?"

"He's going to be okay," he said. "As you can see, we've started to run an IV and we're monitoring his blood sugar levels." He flashed a smile at Hank. "He's been a good patient, Ms. Young. There were quite a few of us fussing and poking him and he took it in stride. Not all kids are so tough in here."

Susan's gaze flickered to Hank's. "I'm proud of you, son," she said. "You're really growing up."

Hank broke into a wide smile. "I told you I was."

While she was proud of her son's behavior, she wasn't near as proud of her own. "Dr. Kent, what happened? I promise, I didn't think he was doing anything out of the ordinary.… He was playing kickball outside with some kids this afternoon."

"Maybe that was it. Sometimes strong physical activity can lower a child's blood glucose levels."

Guilt slammed her hard. Once again, she hadn't been paying enough attention to everything. When was she ever going to be the parent Hank needed? Surely by now most parents would have gotten the hang of all the testing strips and diet and exercise guidelines? "I thought he was fine," she said weakly. "Oh, Hank, I'm so sorry."

The doctor shook his head. "Please don't feel guilty. The body isn't a machine. Sometimes things don't happen right away. And he's better now. We're going to keep him here another hour, and a nurse is going to come in and talk with you, but then I'm going to say you will be free to go home. Hank, I have a feeling you'll sleep better in your own room."

"I will."

"I will, too. Thank you, Doctor," Susan murmured.

"I really do feel better," Hank announced with a toothy grin.

She almost laughed, he looked to be taking the whole

episode in stride. "Hank, we're going to have to really watch how much you exercise. We're going to have to really watch everything you do."

The nurse who came in heard her words and patted her on the shoulder. "Ms. Young," she said. "Please don't be too hard on yourself. Plenty of people have episodes, even adults who've had diabetes for years. Monitoring carbs and glucose is a constant job."

"I still feel like I should be doing better for him."

"I promise, learning to live with diabetes is difficult. Pretty soon things will get easier for you both. Y'all are doing just fine."

"I promise I'm better, Mom," Hank said.

"I'm glad." And she was glad. But she also felt more alone than ever before. She was alone, and she wasn't handling anything very well. Definitely not balancing Hank and work.

Not her love life. Something had to be done. Perhaps coming here, attempting to start over, had been a huge mistake. And though she'd been putting off the phone call she needed to make to Mr. Norton, Susan resolved to finally make that call on Monday morning.

She needed to quit hoping Cal would call and apologize, quit hoping everything was going to run like clockwork, and make plans to move back to Cincinnati.

Home, she reminded herself stubbornly.

Funny how Cincinnati didn't feel like home any longer.

LATE THAT NIGHT, LONG AFTER Hank had gone to bed and she'd taken a shower, Susan called Betsy. "Do you have time to talk?"

"Sure. Want me to come over?"

"No…I just need someone to talk things through with."

"What's up?"

"Betsy, I think I need to go back home," she murmured, feeling like a failure all the while.

"Home, like Ohio?"

"Yes."

"What happened?"

"Hank had a bad night. I think he needs to be near a bigger medical center. And maybe I need to be near more family."

"Susan, how come I didn't even know about this? Why didn't you call me?"

"I don't know. I didn't want to bother you."

"Well, it's sure as heck going to bother me if you up and leave Electra. I like having you as my neighbor."

"Betsy, really? Even after everything that happened with Gene?"

"Susan, just because we're different doesn't mean we can't be friends."

The rightness of her words made Susan smile. "Maybe you're right."

"I know I am. Now, listen, you can tell me all the gory details about Hank tomorrow, but listen to me here—it would be a huge mistake to run away."

"Like I said, if I was in Ohio, I'd be near family."

"You would, but we both know you're not all that close to them. No, it's much better for you to stay here."

"I'm not sure…"

"What about Cal? I'm sure he'd miss you."

"Betsy, things between us are kind of over, if you want to know the truth." Actually, that was putting it mildly. Cal hadn't even stopped by to say hello when he and his brother had picked up Cal Sr. to take him home to their ranch.

"I saw the way he was looking at you at Bob's. He cares. He'll come around. Men are just slow that way."

Betsy sounded so sure and matter-of-fact, Susan smiled. "I had no idea you were so smart about life."

"That's why you need to stick around Electra, Susan. There's a whole host of things you're just finding out about folks here. Please say you'll think about it."

"I will, but I can't promise anything. Something needs to change, and it might just have to be me."

On her end of the phone, Betsy sighed. "If you want to talk more tomorrow, call me."

"I will. And thanks for listening."

"Don't say that. We're friends. And we'll get through this just fine. I know it as sure as I know a ring from Gene is going to come my way…sooner or later."

When Susan hung up, she shook her head in wonder. That old adage really was true…the more things changed, the more they stayed the same.

Chapter Twenty-One

Kay Lawson's jaw went slack when Susan told her the news. "But, Susan, I thought you were fitting in so well."

"I was. I mean, I do like being here. I just don't think staying is a possibility. I really don't think I can handle this job the way you need me to...and be there for Hank, too."

"But it's only been a few months." Kay worried her bottom lip. "It's been so nice, knowing that you're here. Have I been taking advantage of you?"

"No. I was doing my job. I was doing what you hired me to do. But doing that job well means I haven't been doing my other one so well. I've let Hank down."

"Perhaps you could cut back your hours. We could do that for a bit."

"That sounds like heaven, but it would bring up a whole batch of other problems. I need this job to support myself. I need to work full-time." Though she hadn't wanted to bring up the opportunity, she added, "Plus, I was offered a promotion at my old job."

"But I didn't think you were happy there?"

"I wasn't, but things have changed there. And maybe I have, too. If I go back to Ohio, I can ask my family to help some. Hank's needs have to come first."

Standing up, Kay walked around the desk and wrapped an arm around Susan's shoulders. "Susan, do you trust me?"

"Yes."

"Then please give yourself more time to think about this. I'll do some thinking, too. Together, we're going to come up with some answers. You are too important to our community here to let you go without a fight."

"But—"

"Please, Susan? We don't have employees who leave after just a few months. I want you to stay. Please give us all some time."

"All right," she said reluctantly. After all, she didn't really feel as though she had a choice. She owed Kay a lot.

"Okay, then. Go on home and take the rest of the day off."

"That's not necessary."

"I think it might be. Go home and relax, dear. Hank might have had a bad episode, but you took an emotional toll, too. Don't discount that."

"All right. Thank you."

Susan grabbed her purse and rushed out of the building. More than ever, she was so confused.

But even more than that, she knew beyond a doubt that she was so tired. So tired of trying to be everything all by herself.

For just a little while, she had thought life might be different in Electra. But really nothing had changed. Once again, a man didn't stay when things weren't great.

And she ended up having to pick up the pieces.

ONLY A CHANCE CONVERSATION with Gwen had clued Cal in that Hank had had an emergency. After trying Susan's cell phone and getting no answer, he ignored all the work on his desk and ran to his truck.

"Where you going?" Jarred called out.

"To find Susan. And don't even think about saying a word against her."

Jarred rubbed his jaw. "Believe me, I won't. Besides, when I made the mistake of talking to Dad about her, he railed at me for a solid hour. Then Serena did, too."

"Oh, yeah?"

"Yeah. According to Dad, Susan Young is a mixture of Mother Teresa and Mary Poppins. And Serena, she said I can be the biggest idiot alive."

Cal waited for Jarred to add something snarky. "And?"

Jarred held up his hands in surrender. "And nothing! You were right. So is Dad. I acted like a jerk. And acted like you needed protecting—which you do not. I'm sorry."

Pulling open the driver's-side door, Cal nodded. "Glad we got that settled." He drove off before Jarred could say another word. They'd have time enough later to talk more and to smooth things over between them.

At the moment, he didn't want to do a thing but see Susan. To make sure that she was okay.

It took him twenty minutes to get to the Lodge. Walking into the air-conditioned building, he pulled a handkerchief out of his back pocket and rubbed it over his forehead.

Paula looked up in surprise when he approached. "Hey, Junior. Your dad went home last week, didn't he? Is everything okay?"

"He's good. I'm, uh, here to see Susan."

"Oh, honey, I'm sorry. She's already gone on home."

"Is she sick? Or is it Hank?"

"No, I think they're both doing all right now." Her voice lowered. "But I'm afraid her days might be numbered here."

"She said that?"

"No…but I heard it through the grapevine. It would be

a shame if she left, wouldn't it? She fits in great here. Just like a glove."

He couldn't have said that better himself. "Thanks, Paula."

"Good luck finding her," she called out as he strode back out into the heat.

Getting into his truck, he decided to go to her apartment. If she wasn't there, well, then he would just wait for her. Sooner or later, she was going to show up. And then he'd see what was the matter. He was concerned about Hank, and about her, too. Concerned enough to realize that he wanted to help her if he could.

Even just for a little while.

Luckily, he saw her car parked right in front of her condo. Two raps on her door brought them face-to-face again.

"Cal? What are you doing here?"

She looked so shocked to see him, his heart practically stopped.

But, of course, it was no less than he deserved. He'd been so worried about getting hurt again that he'd distanced himself from her.

Without a word of explanation. "As soon as I heard about Hank, I came looking for you."

"Ah. Well, don't worry. He's better now."

When she looked ready to slam the door in his face, he held on to the wood. "Susan, listen. I'm sorry," he blurted. "I'm so sorry I acted like such an ass when Jarred was giving you grief. I'm sorry I called you on my cell phone and told you I wanted a break. Will you ever be able to forgive me?"

She shrugged. "Your words hurt, Cal, but a lot of this was my fault. I should have told you about that job offer first. Not Jarred."

Unable to be so close to her and not touch her, Cal reached out for her hands. After a moment of resistance, she relaxed and folded her hands around his. "I wish you would have called me last night about Hank, Sue."

"You didn't want to get close."

"I was hurt that you were thinking about leaving—and there was nothing I could do about it." He shook his head. "I'm an idiot, but that's nothing new. I should have talked to you more about Christy. About how she made me not trust women."

She bit her lip. "I…I've had trust issues, too. Greg left when things were too hard."

He suddenly realized they were standing in her doorway with the door wide open. "Can I come in and stay awhile? Just as friends?"

After a pause, she nodded. "Sure. If…if that's what you want."

"I want."

After she closed the door behind her, Susan led the way to her little living room. When she sat on the couch, he joined her there and clasped her hands again, needing to touch her.

"So…what happened?"

"Hank had an episode. He passed out. I thought he was going into a coma or something." She shrugged. "I'm trying to do the best I can, but I guess he had too much exercise and I didn't check his insulin levels." Raising her eyes to his, he saw they were filled with tears. "It was awful."

There was only one thing to do. He wrapped his arms around her. "Shh. It's gonna be okay, honey."

"Cal—"

"Please, just let me hold you. We'll figure out everything else soon enough."

Little by little, the muscles in her body relaxed against him. After a moment, she pressed her face against his chest. "For a moment there, I thought I had lost my boy," she said. Sobs racked her. He gently rubbed her back, and realized how their communication had gotten so messed up.

Like a fool, he'd let old problems, gossip, his brother mess everything up.

He could have saved them so much pain if he'd only been more patient and let things happen instead of trying to control everything.

As her tears dampened his shirt, he closed his eyes and wished he could turn back time, or at least suddenly know the right thing to say to her.

As it was, he felt her slipping away from him.

"We'll make things better, Sue. I promise. I won't let you down."

With a hiccup, she pulled away. "There's nothing you can do. See, the thing is, I'm out of options, Cal. I thought I could do everything myself, but I can't. In fact, I'm doing a pretty horrible job of it."

"I don't think so."

"That's where you're wrong. I need to stay at work in order to do a good job, but I can't put in any more hours without sacrificing Hank. I just can't do it all. I've been trying, but I can't."

"Don't try anymore," he blurted. "Lean on me."

"What?"

"Lean on me, even if you only want me to be your friend. Lean on me. I'll support you. I'm strong enough."

Cradled in his arms, Susan felt herself tense. Oh, his words were the stuff of dreams.

They were everything she'd hoped to hear one day. The very words she knew that could make her fall in love.

But what if Cal changed his mind again? She had Hank. And she couldn't play games with his emotions. Hank already had plenty to deal with, given his adjustment to Texas and having diabetes.

What would happen if Cal suddenly decided she was too much for him? That he wanted, needed an easier woman? That he wasn't ready for a commitment…again?

She would be devastated. But Hank, well, Hank would be crushed.

She moved to the end of the couch. "Cal…I think we need to wait."

"For what?"

"We need to make sure that we're not just imagining that we have something. We need to be sure."

"Susan, I told you. I was wrong. That night at the drive-in…what we had was really special."

"That was nice…but it wasn't love, was it?"

"It could have been." Something shadowed his eyes. Then he said, "And maybe it is love now."

She wanted to believe him. But she just wasn't sure. "I've already lived through more than my share of could-have-beens. I don't need that again. I really think I should leave here and go back home to Cincinnati."

"Is that what you want to do? Run away?"

"It wouldn't be running." But even as she said that, she knew it was.

But sometimes, running was the only option. "Thank you for stopping by. But it's time for you to go."

"You sure?"

All she had to do was think of Hank. Of how hurt he would be to have Cal, and then lose him. "I'm positive."

Chapter Twenty-Two

All the time he'd been trying to fuss over his brother and supervise his sister and care for his father—and figure out why it hadn't driven him crazy—one truth had come to surface. He liked being needed.

With some dismay, Cal realized he liked people depending on him. It made him feel useful. As far as he was concerned, he had broad shoulders and a good mind. He had more than enough room in his heart to bear the burdens of someone else.

He wished Susan could have seen that.

But instead of realizing that all he had wanted to do was help her out with her problems, she'd pushed him away.

And now he was likely going to be alone for the rest of his life.

Sipping his iced tea, he opened up the latest financial report that had been delivered from the bank and began reading it carefully.

Only the unmistakable sound of a Riddell man in boots walking down the hall jarred him from his focus.

"Trent?"

"You better believe it," his brother answered with a sassy grin. "Whoa. Look at you! You look like death warmed over."

"Thanks."

"I never thought I'd live to see the day you'd be moping around the house. You're the guy who has always seemed like he could run the world by 8:00 a.m. Now, though, it looks like your world has plumb fallen apart."

It pretty much had, but Trent didn't need to know that. Standing, he said, "What are you doing here?"

"I heard you might be needing me."

"What?"

"I called him," Jarred said, coming up behind Trent. "I told him to get on home and help me straighten you out."

Trent walked over and faced Cal. "Don't say a word about me not coming over here. It wasn't easy flying with a cast on, let me tell you that. Everyone at the airport seemed to enjoy inspecting me a little too much to make sure my cast wasn't a terrorist threat."

"I'm not going to say a word." Then Cal broke his promise. "But you shouldn't have come."

"I couldn't help it. You needed me."

"I was getting along fine...."

Trent grinned. "No, you weren't! You need advice. And you need it bad."

"What advice do you think you can give me?"

"Only that you need to do everything you can to keep hold of Susan."

"You don't even know her."

"I've heard enough about her from people who do," Trent retorted. "And they say she's the best thing that's ever happened to you."

Cal looked at Jarred. "You told Trent that?"

"I did." Looking a bit shamefaced, Jarred added, "Well, I did after Serena reminded me."

"Somehow I've completely messed things up."

"No, you haven't," Jarred said easily. "All you have to do is say you're sorry."

Cal scratched his head. "Really? I don't think that will be enough."

Trent shook his head in wonder. "For a guy so smart with numbers, you're as dumb as bricks with women. Of course saying you're sorry ain't enough."

Cal glared at him. "Okay, Einstein. What's your advice?"

"The obvious," Trent declared. "Call up reinforcements. Talk to her boss or her friends…and get their advice."

Jarred winked. "But my advice is to do it quick. Before it's too late."

SUSAN WAS LATER THAN USUAL getting to work, which was exactly *not* how she had wanted to start her last week at the Lodge.

Of course, a lot of things had happened that morning that had been out of her control. Hank had been cranky, slower than usual getting up and eating his cereal. She spilled coffee on her white skirt not ten minutes after she'd slipped it on, which meant a whole outfit change.

Then just minutes after dropping off Hank, she realized she was almost out of gas. And getting gas wasn't an easy thing in Electra. Filling up a tank necessitated going down the highway for five miles in the opposite direction, waiting in line at one of the five pumps that worked and visiting with everyone there or being seen as rude.

It was going to be one of the many things she would not miss about small-town life, Susan sternly told herself. Yes, it was better to think that way instead of remembering that for the first time, she'd actually known half the people at the gas station.

And that every one of them had asked about Hank.

No, she definitely was not going to think about that.

Instead, she grabbed her purse, slammed her car door and walked briskly into the main entrance.

As the cool breeze of central air-conditioning hit her in the face, Paula waved her down.

"Where's the fire?"

Susan skidded to a stop. "What are you talking about?"

"Honey, you're running in here like flames are about to burn your butt. Are you okay?"

"No. I'm late."

"For the first time since you started. What happened?"

"Everything that could have gone wrong today did."

A secret smile lit the receptionist's face. "I wouldn't say that."

"Why not?"

"I could tell you, but I think you'd rather see what I mean. Go on down to your office. There's something waiting for you there."

Susan frowned. "What is it? Another crisis happen with one of the staff?"

"I'm not telling. Go on now," Paula said.

As soon as she was about to turn down the hallway, it suddenly dawned on her that things were a lot different in the front office than usual. No residents were hovering nearby, wondering when the mail was going to be delivered. No one was waiting to speak to her.

Even the four women sitting on the pair of couches across the way in the main lobby seemed to be strangely silent. As were the trio of folks sipping coffee near the coatrack. Recognizing Rosa Ventura, Susan delayed going to her office a little longer. "What's going on?"

"Nothing, dear. I'm just having my coffee in here today."

Rosa didn't have her coffee just anywhere. Everyone in the building knew Rosa sat in the garden room and sipped her two cups while working on her morning crossword. But when she only crossed her legs and looked very haughtily at her, Susan pushed her confusion away and went on in.

And then stood in the doorway and gaped. There, taking up almost her whole desk, was the most beautiful arrangement of roses she'd ever seen. Two—no, three—dozen stems of different shades of pink stood proudly in a gorgeous cut-crystal vase.

Leaning up against the vase was a square envelope. Her name was printed neatly across the front.

Slowly, she approached the bouquet, almost afraid to blink. Instead, she closed her eyes and breathed deep. Oh, the aroma was heavenly.

"Aren't you going to open the card and see who they're from?" Kay called out from her door.

"Kay?" She turned to her boss. "What's going on?"

"Quite a lot." A dimple appeared in Kay's cheek as she pointed toward Susan's front window—the one that looked out toward the main hallway.

Susan pivoted, and then stared, dumbstruck. It looked as if half the people who either worked or lived in the Lodge were gathered around that glass…and they were looking right back at her, grinning.

Huh. Her flowers seemed to be the biggest news of the day. Had Cal sent them to her? She started to feel all tingly at the thought.

"Open the card, Susan," Kay prompted with a smile.

"All right. Here we go," she said, picking up the envelope and neatly pulling up the flap.

We Want You To Stay.

She felt her mouth drop open as she read the card, and then read it again. There, covering the bottom and back of the card had to be at least fifty signatures. Disappointment that Cal hadn't sent the bouquet dissipated as she realized just how many people right there at the Lodge had contributed to her present.

And with that, a different type of warmth floated through her. One filled from knowing that she was accepted. Looking at the window, she motioned everyone in.

That was all the prodding anyone needed! Soon her small office was packed with people, young and old. Each one smiling a thousand-watt grin.

Susan couldn't help but grin, too. "You all bought me flowers?"

"We sure did," Paula said as she pushed her way forward. "We wanted to do something grand."

"Roses are special, don't you think?" Rosa asked from her wheelchair by the door.

Tears pricked her eyes. "It's all grand. And special. Especially the note. But why did y'all do this?"

Paula answered that one. "It's kind of obvious, I think. We don't want you to move away. We like you. We think you fit right in."

Kay grinned as she stepped closer. "Word spread like wildfire around here on Friday when you left. Everyone got together and tried to come up with the perfect gift."

"You mean bribe," Paula teased.

"Whatever you want to call it, we knew you like flowers," Paula pointed out. "And, well, we wanted to give you a gift you couldn't refuse."

As laughter followed Paula's remark, Susan playfully hugged her vase close. Well, as close as she could. "Oh, don't worry, I certainly won't refuse these. They're the most beautiful flowers I've ever seen in my life! But they sure weren't necessary."

As the room quieted down, Kay said quietly, "I know

you've got some things you have to deal with. But, we'd rather you stay here and work them out than leave us."

"We want to help you out with Hank, too," Paula said. "I already checked with the school-bus system and guess what? Hank can be dropped off right here after school."

Rosa nodded. "And all of us are going to take turns helping him with schoolwork and eating healthy snacks when you can't."

Susan couldn't believe what she was hearing. "But Hank isn't your job. He's not your responsibility...."

Kay placed her hands on her hips. "Susan Young, don't you get it yet? You're more to us than just a worker. You're part of our family here. We want to help."

Susan was embarrassed to realize that the tears she'd tried so hard to still were now falling down her cheeks. How different this place was, compared to her old job!

Why hadn't she realized that? Why hadn't she taken what Betsy had said to heart all those weeks ago? There really was a whole lot more to feeling secure than just a good paycheck!

"You all mean that?" she asked.

"Of course we do," Paula replied. "Your smiles around here have made us smile. Your caring ways have been something to look forward to."

"Besides, now that Calvin's gone, no one else wants to play gin with me," Rosa said.

"Please tell us you won't make us play cards with her again," one of the aides murmured.

As the room erupted again into laughter, Susan was aware of another feeling permeating the air. Expectation. Everyone was waiting for her answer.

Suddenly, she felt as though she had just come home—well, to a home that only good friends could give a person.

It was made up of people who cared about her and gave her a reason to get up each morning.

It was startling to realize that although she had felt that way about the Electra Lodge, these people had viewed her in much the same way. They wanted her in their lives.

They needed her there.

What more could she ask for? She had a wonderful son who meant the world to her, and these wonderful people. It was okay if she didn't have Cal Riddell, too.

One day, maybe, she'd be brave enough to risk another relationship. But until that day came, she was going to be satisfied with doing the best she could, and being thankful for good friends who cared about her.

Wiping a stray tear from her eye, she looked around the room. "Thank you all. No one...no one has ever done so much for me. Ever. These flowers, this card—and all of you being here—it means the world to me."

"So, did it work?" Rosa asked.

"Like a charm," Susan said with a laugh. "Kay, you better look out, because you're not getting rid of me now. I'm finally going to put down roots. I'm here to stay."

As a spurt of clapping lit the air, Susan moved from staff member to resident as everyone rushed forward to offer their best wishes and she offered her thanks.

After almost an hour, everyone but Rosa left. Susan was a little surprised by that. She enjoyed her conversations with the older lady. And they'd definitely shared a few laughs.

But Rosa had never come to her office and settled in for so long.

But maybe there was another reason? But Susan didn't want to push, so she just stacked up some paperwork and bided her time.

And, finally, Rosa spoke. Crossing her arms over her

ample chest, she looked Susan in the eye. "I can't tell you how glad I am that you decided to stay here."

"I can't tell you how glad I feel that I *can* stay. I've been really struggling with the right thing to do."

"I think we'll all enjoy spending more time with Hank."

"He'll like it, too."

"'Course, I imagine there's someone else he'll enjoy being with, too."

Susan knew who had put that gleam in the lady's eyes. "Cal?"

"The very one. How are things going with him?"

"I'm not sure. I don't know if we'll ever get back to how we were."

"Ah, trust."

"You read my mind," she said sheepishly.

"No, I haven't been mind reading. Instead, I've been talking to his father."

"Mr. Riddell?"

"The very one. We've gotten pretty close, you know. He's been worried about his boy." Her gaze strayed away from Susan's for a moment, then a new glint appeared. "I think you should give that Cal Riddell another chance."

"There's nothing to give him a chance about. We're just in different places in our lives."

"But still, look what happened here today. Sometimes it's best to look at the big picture, you know. To think about how you *want* things to be instead of just getting stuck on what is."

"I'll remember that."

"See that you do," she said softly as she rolled her wheelchair out of the room. "And you should probably do that sooner rather than later."

Susan looked up and nearly stopped breathing. Cal stood in the doorway, holding his hat in his hands.

"What are you doing here, Cal?"

"I had a conversation with a certain bossy receptionist. She informed me that I better get my act together...or else."

"Paula called you?"

"No, I called her for advice."

"And she gave it to you?"

"Kind of. She passed the phone around and a whole slew of people gave me advice. Although their advice was good, what really mattered was how I felt. And I knew I had to see you, Sue."

As his gaze settled on her, Susan felt her cheeks heat. Then she noticed he looked mildly uncomfortable. "Are you okay?"

"Oh, yeah. It's just the roses."

"I think they're beautiful. Everyone here got them for me." Her words stilled as she watched him take a deep breath and almost brace himself before stepping forward. "Are you allergic to them or something?"

"No. It's just, ah, my mother loved roses. I'm glad you do, too."

"This bouquet, it seems like too much, you know? I don't deserve it."

"You do. Of course you do."

"But they were so expensive."

"People just wanted you to see how much they care. They're trying to do something to show you that they care about you...like you care about them. You've pulled them close with your smiles. With your warm, caring manner."

"I don't know about that...."

"I do," he replied. "I watched you when I've stopped by and visited. And I know, because you've pulled me in, too."

"I did?"

"You did. Just like a fish." Looking behind him at the

picture window, he held out a hand. "Can we go outside for a bit? Go for a walk?"

Her heart constricted. Oh, that was such a Cal thing to say. So formal in so many ways. Hesitant, and yet tough. "Of course."

His gaze warmed as he led her out.

Paula winked when they passed. Behind Paula, Kay simply looked on, silently watching, a bemused expression in her eyes.

After they exited the front doors, they both turned right, then walked out to the wide path. Usually it was filled with people strolling, but today, aside from a young couple pushing a baby stroller, they were alone.

The heat of the sun beat on their shoulders and warmed their faces. Beside her, Cal breathed deep. Seconds passed. Then finally, he spoke. "Here's the deal, Sue. All my life, I imagined that falling in love would be a sudden thing. Like a bolt of lightning or something. No doubts. But instead, I've been falling for you by stops and starts. Now I can't stay away."

What was he saying? Had he mentioned love? "Cal, did you just say you loved me?"

He rolled his eyes. "Susan, I'm no good with flowery things, with talking fancy. I'm a pretty simple guy, when all's said and done. I love my family, and I like being needed. I'm good with math, but not with crowds. And…I love you."

The cold casing that had covered her heart for years cracked and chipped away. Right then and there, she knew it was time to stop shielding herself from pain and finally live again. And love. "I like to laugh, and I love old people. I love my son, and I like being needed, too. And, Cal Riddell Jr., I love you, too."

He blinked, then slowly smiled. "Yeah?"

"Yeah."

He stopped walking. And, because they were alone, and, she guessed, because he was, well, Cal, he knelt down in front of her and Main Street, too.

As she stood there, half-stunned and looking down at him, knowing that the whole world had pretty much stopped, too, she whispered, "Cal?"

"Hush, now. I'm going to do this right." He took a deep breath. "Susan, would you do me the very great honor of becoming my wife?"

"Of course," she said, reaching down and grabbing his hands to pull him up. And then, because she couldn't help herself, she stepped forward and wrapped her hands around his neck and pressed herself against him.

She kissed him. A big ol' Texas-size kiss, with lips open and hardly an inch of space between their bodies.

When they parted, Cal gazed into her eyes and grinned. "What was that for?"

"For everything," she said simply. "Just, for everything."

"For everything, huh?" Cal draped an arm around her shoulders as they started walking again. "'Everything' might just be enough."

* * * * *

*Be sure to look for Shelley Galloway's
next book in the* MEN OF RED RIVER *trilogy,
MY CHRISTMAS COWBOY!
Bull rider and ladies' man Trent Riddell
finally gets tamed....*

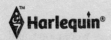
Harlequin®

American ★ Romance®

COMING NEXT MONTH

Available September 13, 2011

#1369 MONTANA SHERIFF
American Romance's Men of the West
Marie Ferrarella

#1370 THE BULL RIDER'S TWINS
Callahan Cowboys
Tina Leonard

#1371 STAND-IN MOM
Creature Comforts
Megan Kelly

#1372 BACHELOR DAD
Fatherhood
Roxann Delaney

HARCNM0811

REQUEST YOUR FREE BOOKS!
2 FREE NOVELS PLUS 2 FREE GIFTS!

LOVE, HOME & HAPPINESS

HARI1B

New York Times *and* USA TODAY *bestselling author*
Maya Banks presents a brand-new miniseries

PREGNANCY & PASSION

When four irresistible tycoons face
the consequences of temptation.

Book 1—*ENTICED BY HIS FORGOTTEN LOVER*

Available September 2011 from Harlequin® Desire®!

Rafael de Luca had been in bad situations before. A crowded ballroom could never make him sweat.

These people would never know that he had no memory of any of them.

He surveyed the party with grim tolerance, searching for the source of his unease.

At first his gaze flickered past her, but he yanked his attention back to a woman across the room. Her stare bored holes through him. Unflinching and steady, even when his eyes locked with hers.

Petite, even in heels, she had a creamy olive complexion. A wealth of inky-black curls cascaded over her shoulders and her eyes were equally dark.

She looked at him as if she'd already judged him and found him lacking. He'd never seen her before in his life. Or had he?

He cursed the gaping hole in his memory. He'd been diagnosed with selective amnesia after his accident four months ago. Which seemed like complete and utter bull. No one got amnesia except hysterical women in bad soap operas.

With a smile, he disengaged himself from the group

around him and made his way to the mystery woman.

She wasn't coy. She stared straight at him as he approached, her chin thrust upward in defiance.

"Excuse me, but have we met?" he asked in his smoothest voice.

His gaze moved over the generous swell of her breasts pushed up by the empire waist of her black cocktail dress.

When he glanced back up at her face, he saw fury in her eyes.

"Have we *met?*" Her voice was barely a whisper, but he felt each word like the crack of a whip.

Before he could process her response, she nailed him with a right hook. He stumbled back, holding his nose.

One of his guards stepped between Rafe and the woman, accidentally sending her to one knee. Her hand flew to the folds of her dress.

It was then, as she cupped her belly, that the realization hit him. She was pregnant.

Her eyes flashing, she turned and ran down the marble hallway.

Rafael ran after her. He burst from the hotel lobby, and saw two shoes sparkling in the moonlight, twinkling at him.

He blew out his breath in frustration and then shoved the pair of sparkly, ultrafeminine heels at his head of security.

"Find the woman who wore these shoes."

Will Rafael find his mystery woman?
Find out in Maya Banks's passionate new novel
ENTICED BY HIS FORGOTTEN LOVER
Available September 2011 from Harlequin® Desire®!

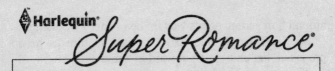

Love and family secrets collide in
a powerful new trilogy from

Linda Warren

Blood is thicker than oil

Coming August 9, 2011.

The Texan's Secret

Before Chance Hardin can join his brothers in
their new oil business, he must reveal a secret
that could tear their family apart. And his
desire for family has never been stronger, all
because of beautiful Shay Dumont.
A woman with a secret of her own....

The Texan's Bride
(October 11, 2011)

The Texan's Christmas
(December 6, 2011)

www.Harlequin.com

HSR71723